THE MIDNIGHT FLAME

RITE WORLD: LIGHTGROVE WITCHES
BOOK 3

JULIANA HAYGERT

COPYRIGHT

AUTHOR'S NOTE

I hope you enjoy reading *The Midnight Flame*!

Don't forget to sign up for my Newsletter to find out about new releases, cover reveals, giveaways, and more!

If you want to see exclusive teasers, help me decide on covers, read excerpts, talk about books, etc, join my reader group on Facebook: Juliana's Club!

1

"She's awake!"

I heard the words, but their meaning didn't register through the fog in my brain. My eyes fluttered open, but a headache pounded around my skull, making me groan in pain with each flash of light floating past my lashes. The pain in my limbs buzzed into a crescendo.

Holy shit, what had I—?

I sat up with a jerk, suddenly remembering what had happened before I blacked out.

Pain ricocheted through my body and my eyes stung at the bright light pointed directly at my face. I rose a trembling hand to cover the light, and realized my hands were handcuffed.

Sluggish and weak, I blinked, waiting for my eyes to adjust to the light, and took in my surroundings. I was seated on a small, hard cot on a dirty, rough floor in the corner of a tiny cell. Three stone walls, no windows, and one wall made of thick metal bars from top to bottom.

On the other side of the bars, a man in dark clothes and hard eyes stared at me as if I were the plague poisoning the Earth.

A Brotherhood of Purity member.

My chest squeezed. Holy shit ... I really had been captured. Panic flowered inside of me, my breath growing shallow. What was I going to do? How was I going to get out of here? With the fog in my mind and the pain in my body, I wasn't going anywhere. Not yet, at least.

For now, I had to swallow my fear and hope they wouldn't kill me before I could recover and escape. I refused die by their hands. That couldn't be my destiny.

Heavy footsteps echoed down the hallway, and four men appeared in front of my cell. I fought the urge to recoil and faced them. The five men looked the same: a military buzz cut, dark hair, hard expressions, and the same black clothes, though none of them wore the red cloaks now. The only variations between them were their heights and build, and their complexions varied from paper white to chestnut brown. One had a faint five o'clock shadow, another one had a nasty scar across his left cheek, and a third one wore thin-framed glasses.

"Finally," the tallest one said, a snarl in his tone. "Bring her." He turned, walking away.

The scarred one reached for the metal bars and unlocked an almost seamless door. He opened it wide and took a step back. "Come."

I hesitated.

"Come or I'll drag you out."

I looked down at my cuffed hands. Though I couldn't

feel it, I was sure these cuffs had a numbing spell preventing me from using my magic. Even if I could, would that be enough against five Brotherhood members? And those were just the ones I could see. If I fought now, I would get more tired and hurt and I would anger them. For now, I needed to be patient. Brave.

I pushed to my feet and my vision blackened. I swayed but caught myself before kissing the floor in front of these men. They snickered at me, as if disappointed. With gritted teeth, I placed one foot in front of the other and did my best to ignore the pain and soreness shooting through my legs and my back. My hands shook with the effort, but I schooled my face to remain expressionless. Cool. In control.

If only my insides felt the same.

I stepped out of the cell and the four men surrounded me. The fear in my chest spiked, and I sucked in a sharp breath, trying to quell the tide of adrenaline.

Fight, flight, or freeze.

There was no option here.

I followed the two men in the front as they led me down the hallway. Five cells lined the hall, and none of them were occupied. As we left the hallway, crossed a small room with two more Brotherhood members, and entered a large room, I kept telling myself I would find a way to escape. Otherwise, the despair blooming in my chest would overtake me.

I looked around the room as the men guided me to the center—large, tall, and wide enough to be an abandoned church, but there were no pews, no altar, no crosses. The walls were painted dark, and a handful of thick pillars lined the center. Thin windows adorned the walls some fifteen feet high, letting the faint light of the fading sunshine through.

Wait ... I had been captured around midnight. It was already evening the next day.

"What day is it?" I asked, my voice hoarse. Shit, my throat was parched.

The scarred man looked up to the window. "If you're wondering how long you've been here ... it's been almost two days."

I balked, nearly tripping on my feet. Two days? So ... it was freaking Tuesday. I hadn't showed up for classes on Monday at the Light Castle or at Towland. Had Moira come after me? Had she reported I was missing? Was the Light Order searching for me?

If yes, then it was only a matter of time until they found me, right?

I hung on to that piece of hope, especially when we arrived in the center of the room. A witch's circle had been drawn on the floor with white chalk, along with four runes I didn't recognize. Two short stone pillars were in the center, and once the men shoved me inside the circle, I found out their purpose. The Brotherhood members unshackle my hands, just to shackle them again, one wrist to each pillar. And because both pillars couldn't have been three feet tall, I had to kneel on the cold, rough, dark floor.

The four Brotherhood members retreated from the circle and stared at me, as if I were a bug inside a jar, and they were the kids who had caught me. Now they needed to decide if they would observe me, play with me, or squash me.

I inhaled slowly, but deeply, and forced my entire self to calm down. If I yelled, if I argued, if I fought, my situation would only get worse.

I heard footsteps again. First it seemed only one person, but soon I saw the fifth man I had met in my cell, and another handful of Brotherhood members behind him.

Oh, shit.

I recoiled into myself but couldn't. I had already promised myself I wouldn't show weakness in front of these bastards, and I physically couldn't move, not with these shackles holding my arms open to my sides.

The man from before, the one who looked like the leader, stopped right in front of me, but outside the circle. He sneered at me. "Comfortable?"

I kept my mouth shut.

"I don't know about comfortable, but she stinks," a bald man said. A wave of faint chuckles echoed through the room. The leader cut the others a cold stare and they all fell silent.

Well, if I was here for two days already, it was probably almost three since I last took a shower. I probably did stink. And right now, I really needed to go to the bathroom.

The leader returned his hard eyes to me. "I don't like wasting time, so I'll get directly to the point. Where're Arianna's things?" I blinked, confused. "Her ashes, necklace, and grimoire. Where are they hidden?"

"What the hell are you talking about?" the words were out of my mouth before I could think better of it.

The man leaned forward, his eyes narrowed. "You know where they are hidden, and you will tell me."

That was insane. "I ... no one knows. They've been lost."

"Then tell me where to find them."

"How the hell would I know?"

He tilted his head. "You can play all you want, Hazel, but you will tell me, one way or another."

"I can't tell you something I don't know!"

He grunted. "My patience runs thin. I'll give you another two days to think about this. But when I come back for you, you better have an answer for me." He turned to the scarred guy to his left. "Leave her here for a few hours, then take her back to her cell."

"Maren, what about—?" Scarred started.

The leader shot him an are-you-going-to-question-me look. "No food for her, just half a glass of water per day."

Scarred nodded and the leader, Maren, walked away. Half of the men followed him, while the other half remained in place, watching me as if I could snap my fingers and disappear at any second.

I wish.

At first, I stared at a blank spot between the two men in my line of sight. I kept my mind busy, distracted, with the many questions swirling around my skull.

The Brotherhood of Purity was after Arianna's ashes, necklace, and grimoire. Why? Was this something new, or had they always tried to find them? It was common knowledge that Arianna could be resurrected if the three items were found and ... and a powerful spell was performed? I mean, no one could bring back the dead. It was just a legend. Right?

The most puzzling part of this, though, was why the hell did they think I knew where the items were? I was an initiate in the Lightgrove coven. I was no one. They should have kidnapped one of the council witches, or at least a full member.

It didn't make any sense.

The pressure of the rough floor on my knees grew unbearable, and my wrists screamed and my arms became numb. I couldn't even move them to make it better.

All thoughts fled my mind and all I could think of was pain.

Maren had said five hours, hadn't he? Shit, it probably hadn't been thirty minutes yet and I already couldn't take any longer.

No, this wasn't how it was supposed to go.

I wouldn't cave in front of these men.

I gritted my teeth, straightened my spine, and thought of fluffy clouds, warm beds, cool pools, and a delicious ice cream that waited for me after this was all said and done.

Mind over matter.

A long time passed, and the guy with glasses handed a twenty-dollar bill to Scarred. "I really thought she would faint after an hour."

Scarred laughed. "Told you she's tougher than she looks."

A third one tsked. "Wait for it. She'll surrender soon."

"No, she won't." Scarred stared at me, a wicked glint in his dark eyes. "Will you?"

They all laughed.

Several colorful words rose in my throat, but I clamped my lips and swallowed them back. Damn it!

I inhaled deeply, closed my eyes, and tuned them out.

I endured like that for as long as I could. Around me, the men moved, chatted, waited, teased, talked … but I was determined to not look at them again. Not yet.

However, after a while, the exhaustion and the pain became too much. I couldn't feel my arms, I couldn't feel my legs, my head swam, and when I tried opening my eyes again, I failed.

Then, I passed out.

2

IT WAS HARD TO TELL TIME. THE CELL HAD NO WINDOWS, BUT I thought there was one at the end of the hallway. I had seen dim light coming from that way a few times, and it reminded me of the sun setting, but I never saw it rising. Most of the time, this place was dark, cold, and creepy.

I was almost glad I spent most of my time sleeping, too weak to care, or do anything else.

I was brought a sip of water a couple of times a day and was allowed to go to a common bathroom three times a day—at least, that was how many times I thought it was. I couldn't be sure.

The first time I was taken to the bathroom, which was only an open, dirty room with a handful of half-broken stalls and no doors, one of the Brotherhood members stood right in front of me, watching me as I grabbed the waist of my filthy pants to pull it down.

"Are you going to stand there?" I snapped.

"I have to keep an eye on you."

"Can't you give me thirty seconds? Just turn your back at least." I brought my shackled hands up and gestured to the sides. "It's not like I can run away from this place, is it?"

He huffed but conceded. He turned his back to me, but remained there, less than five feet while I gave in and finally peed. Mortified was an understatement.

But that was only the first couple of times. After that, I didn't even care anymore.

I paced my cell, trying to regain my strength, but I was still bruised and sore, and with an empty stomach, I wouldn't last long. There was no fighting exhaustion.

Finally, when it seemed I had been here forever, Scarred brought me food.

"Eat up."

He threw a loaf of bread the size of my fist at my face. Surprised, I didn't catch it and it rolled to the dirty floor. I was delirious with hunger; I didn't care. I knelt, grabbed the bread, and bit a good chunk off.

Scarred chuckled. "Just like a wild animal." He placed a bottle of water on the floor, just past the bars, then crossed his arms and watched me.

Half of the dry, sour bread was already gone, and I knew I would probably throw up eating so fast, but right now, this bread was the best meal I had ever had. When the bread disappeared, I grabbed the water bottle and drank half of it in one gulp. After who knew how long without food and only drinking a sip of water here and there, this meal tasted like heaven.

I held the bottle tight, afraid my weak, trembling hands would let it fall, and I would waste even a drop. I sank to the floor, resting my back against my cot.

"Don't get too comfortable," Scarred said. "You have five minutes to recover, then I'm taking you away."

I stilled. Taking me away? What did he mean?

In the past few days, I hadn't had enough strength to sit up, much less to talk. But now I wanted to know.

"Take me away?" My voice hurt my dry throat. "Where?"

Scarred's brows knotted. "What does it matter to you? You don't have a choice."

All right, it wouldn't be easy to get answers from him, but that didn't mean I needed to give up.

"You're right; I don't have a choice." I took another sip of my water. "But if you're going to kill me, what's the problem with telling me anyway."

"Who said we'll kill you?"

My eyes widened. "You won't?"

"If we want to find Arianna's things, then we need you."

I pushed to my knees and scooted closer to the bars. "Why? Why do you need me? Why do you think I can find them?"

"I've said too much already." Scarred took two steps back. "Shut up and be a good girl."

"But—"

Scarred flew forward, reached through the bars, and grabbed my neck. "I said shut. The. Fuck. Up." He gave it one good squeeze, then let me go.

I gasped as my throat burned and my lungs screamed for air. Fighting the sudden exhaustion that hit me, I inhaled deeply and forced myself to calm down. Panicking and breaking down now wouldn't get me anywhere.

Not a minute later, another handful of Brotherhood members appeared beside Scarred. They opened the cell door and ordered me out. I pushed to my feet and wobbled through the entrance. I could barely keep my head up, much less my entire body. I tripped twice in less than ten seconds. The third time, I tipped over and was sure I would have kissed the floor, if it weren't for the hard grip on my arm that kept me up.

"Useless witch," the man whispered. He kept me as far away as he could while still digging his fingers painfully into my skin.

"When can we get rid of her?" one of them asked, his voice low.

"I don't think we will anytime soon."

"Not until Maren finds out—"

"Quiet!" Scarred snapped.

The Brotherhood of Purity members went silent instantly. Shit. For a second there, I thought I would find out what Maren wanted with Arianna's things.

I wasn't surprised when the men dragged me to the same room as before and chained me to the low pillars. This time, a cry escaped my lips when my knees hit the rough floor and pain spread through my weak body.

Seriously, a few more days like this and I would be dead.

Of pain, of exhaustion, of hunger.

Of frustration and disappointment.

Of heartache.

I didn't know how long I stayed like that ... another day? A few hours? I must have dozed off for a while, because I jerked in alert when Maren walked into the room followed by six other men.

He stopped a few feet in front of me, just outside the circle containing me. The men behind him fanned out, as if positioning themselves for a fight. What? Would they beat up a half-dead witch now? Well, they hunted and killed us. I was sure torture-for-fun wasn't beyond them.

I looked at the men, facing each of them for a few seconds, making sure they saw that even though I was weak, I wasn't afraid of them. At least, on the outside.

Inside, I was trembling like a pebble in an earthquake.

Most men stared back at me with disdain and disgust.

And then I saw the last man.

My eyes widened, my heart clenched, the air fled from my lungs.

"Se—" I clamped my mouth shut when he lifted his head and looked at me.

Sean had been upset with me when I had first seen him, but now he seemed livid. And disgusted, just like the others.

His brothers.

My shoulders slumped forward.

Holy shit, Sean was a member of the Brotherhood of Purity.

He had played me. He probably knew who I was from the beginning. He had used me, and then he had sent his brothers to catch me when all I was trying to do was help his late best friend.

Sean's brows knotted, his jaw clenched, and he averted his eyes, as if he couldn't stare at me anymore.

My heart squeezed again. This hurt much more than the shackles around my wrists, than the rough floor against my knees, than the hunger that drew a hole in my stomach.

A sob rose to my throat, but I swallowed it.

I had been determined to not break in front of any member of the Brotherhood, and I wouldn't start now.

"Ready to talk?" Maren asked, his voice as callous as before.

I snapped my head to him, though a force kept pulling me, wanting me to look at Sean again. Maybe I had imagined him? It couldn't be him. Sean was a human with no knowledge of this.

Right?

I glanced at him for two seconds and my breath caught.

Despite the black robes covering his body, he was still striking with his bright blue eyes, far skin, and his dark brown hair—shaved closed on the sides, and longer on the top. The robe didn't hide how tall and wide and muscular he was, though it did hide all his tattoos.

It was him all right, and it hurt like hell.

I fixed my gaze on Maren, even though I barely saw him through the tears that threatened to spill. I blinked fast, pushing them away.

I won't break down now.

I won't break down now.

"Talk, witch, or you'll be back in that cell for another three days," Maren threatened.

I could barely reason, let alone talk. No ... I pushed Sean to the back of my mind—if I could, I would have pushed him out of my mind, but that was impossible right now—and focused on Maren. I considered being quiet. I knew nothing, but I wanted information, and I would only get it if I spoke.

"I'm up because of these damn chains," I said, my voice thin and frail. My throat hurt. "I can barely stand, and you want me to talk."

He tilted his head. "You're talking."

"I will talk, but first, I want a real meal and a shower ... without your creeps watching me."

Maren shook his head. "I can arrange the meal, but I don't think the shower will be possible."

I knew it was a long shot, but I had to try. He had revealed three days had gone by since I last saw him, plus the two before that. I hadn't had a shower in five days and even I couldn't stand myself.

"I'll take it," I said, my teeth gritted.

Maren nodded. "I'll have a meal brought to you. Meanwhile ... hang in there." He scoffed, as if he were hilarious. "I'll be back later." He turned, walking away.

The six men who had come with him turned and followed him.

Including Sean.

I tried to resist it. I really tried, but I was too weak.

I looked at him as he gave me his back, his eyes always staring straight ahead. Not once did he glance at me.

My breath hitched as he marched out of the room.

And I was left with Scarred and his gang in this dark, cold prison.

3

TWO HOURS LATER, MAREN HAD SENT A GUY WHO COULDN'T have been older than fifteen to bring me a small bowl of watery soup and stale bread. Scarred released one of my arms for me to eat—otherwise he would have to spoon feed me.

I chomped down on my soup, knowing that if this had been served to me anywhere else, in any other time of my life, I wouldn't have even touched. But I was beyond hungry.

The fact that the soup, or the bread earlier, could have been poisoned crossed my mind, but if they wanted me dead, they could have done so five days ago. For some reason, they wanted me alive. Probably to tell them whatever they thought I knew about Arianna's items.

I tried focusing on that—why was I here? How long would they keep me alive? How would I get some of the answers I was looking for from Maren? Because if I focused on the new, raw, and deep pain inside my chest, I would drown in my sorrow within seconds.

Sean was in the Brotherhood of Purity.

How blind and stupid had I been that I hadn't seen it?

I thought long and hard about our time together, the things he had said, what we had done ... but I couldn't find anything suspicious. Had he been so good at his job that I was clueless? Like those sleeper agents who had real lives until they were called upon ... and then they heartlessly killed their spouse and children in the name of their country.

I shuddered and tears filled my eyes again.

The soup and the bread hadn't helped my condition. I still felt weary and too weak to hold myself up for long. It only took a few minutes for my body to slump forward and for me to faint, hanging from my wrists.

———

"WHAT'S THAT?" A VOICE PIERCED THE DARKNESS, AND I jolted awake.

I groaned as I straightened my back, my body sore and my knees and wrists in agonizing pain.

"I don't know," someone else said.

I shook my head once, trying to awaken fully and understand what was happening. It was dark in the room, darker than before. Was it the middle of the night? So, Maren hadn't come for me yet?

"There!" One of the five Brotherhood members in the room pointed to a dark corner.

"I don't see anything," another one said.

"Stop playing around, asshole," a third one snapped. "Just do your job."

The man lowered his arm and slapped his own face. "Sleep might be getting to me. We've been here for hours."

A fourth one nodded. "Our shift is almost over."

"Shh, the witch is awake," the fifth man said.

They all turned to me, their stances ready to attack. I pulled on the chains and groaned as another jolt of pain traveled up my arms. This was pure agony. I had to get out of here. My body would break in three hundred pieces if I stayed in this position for much longer.

Then, out of nowhere, a meow echoed through the room.

The men all look at each other.

"You heard that, right?" one asked.

"I did," another replied.

"But ... a cat? Here? How?"

From the corner of the room, a black cat strolled toward the five Brotherhood members. They all turned to the cat and froze, stunned.

I gawked at the feline ... could it be the same cat?

No, that was crazy.

The cat stopped a few feet from the men and meowed again.

A shadow took shape in the corner of the room, right behind the cat. It moved forward, growing bigger, until he stepped closer and the dim light in the room illuminated his figure.

Sean.

"Now," he said.

A swirl of smoke covered the cat, and a man unfolded from within the smoke. I blinked, wishing I could rub at my eyes. The man was almost as tall as Sean, with black hair, black eyes, and dark olive skin. He wore black slacks and a button-up shirt.

He sneered at the Brotherhood members.

"Meow," he said in a mocking tone.

Then he charged at them.

Sean ran to me.

Panic rose in my chest, and I tried scooting back, but the chains wouldn't allow me to move.

"Hazel," he whispered, falling to his knees in front of me. He reached for my face. "What—?"

I bit at his approaching hands, and he pulled back, alarmed.

"Stay away!" I screamed.

"I'm trying to help you." He moved to one of the pillars and fished a bronze key from the pocket of his pants. "I'm getting you out of here." He unlocked the shackle from the pillar and gently opened it from around my wrist.

I pulled my right arm to my chest, fast, and watched as he moved to the other pillar. Meanwhile, the cat-slash-man fought the Brotherhood members with such grace and speed, he really reminded me of a tiger.

"I ... I don't understand." My left arm fell heavy beside me. Holy shit, everything hurt.

"There's no time to explain." Sean reached for me again, and I slapped his hands away. I groaned, as a jolt of pain assaulted me. "Hazel, please ... I know you're mad at me. You can yell at me all you want, but after we get out of here. Okay?"

I cradled my aching wrists and stared at him. "You're one of them."

With a grunt, Sean shoved a crystal in one of my hands. "Here, absorb its magic. You'll feel better."

I grabbed the crystal. Strong magic pulsed within. "Why—?"

"Holy shit, Hazel. No time for questions." He hooked an arm around my waist and pulled me up. I wanted to step away from him, but the instant I stood upright, my legs became jelly, pain throbbed through every inch of my body. I slumped forward. Sean passed his arms around my back and under my knees and hoisted me to his chest.

"Ready?" he asked, but he wasn't looking at me.

The cat-slash-man landed an impressive kick to the temple of the last of the Brotherhood men, causing him to fall unconscious to the floor.

He dusted something from his shoulder, smoothed his hands down his shirt. "Now, I'm ready."

He looked at me, his dark eyes shining bright. "Hazel, it's nice to finally meet you. I'm Shade."

"You're ..." I couldn't say it.

"The cat, yes," Shade said. "I'll explain everything once we're out of here." He looked around. "This way."

He dashed into the darkness and Sean followed him, carrying me with him. "Take the magic from the crystal, Hazel. You need it."

As they maneuvered through a long, dark hallway, I closed my eyes and inhaled deeply, taking the crystal's magic for myself. Some of the pain in my bones and muscles eased, and I felt like I could even cast a quick spell if needed. This was quite different from being better, but it would do.

With the crystal's magic in my veins, I could even walk. Next time we stopped and Shade looked ahead, I forced my legs down. Sean gently dropped me beside him, and I took two generous steps back.

He closed a hand around my elbow and pulled me toward him under an archway, pressing my body against his. Two men walked down the other side of the hallway, talking in low voices. Patrols.

Sean had saved me from being found out.

Hands splayed on his chest, I looked up and found his face only inches from mine. His eyes locked on mine, and my breath caught.

"No time for that, lovebirds," Shade whispered. "Come on."

He rounded the corner of the dark hallway and disappeared. Sean took my hand in his, tugging me to come with him. As silent as we could, we followed Shade into a wider hallway.

Despite all the emotions swimming freely inside of me, I couldn't help but gawk at this place. We were in an old hotel or office building. Was this the Brotherhood of Purity headquarters? If it was, then I wanted to memorize it so I could give the Lightgrove coven information.

We took narrow steps and emerged into what looked like a large lobby, dark and with many glass windows, and a dozen Brotherhood members.

"Hey! Stop!" one of them yelled before lunging at us.

Sean pulled me behind him, and Shade jumped into the fray as if he was Bruce Lee.

Two men ran toward Sean and me. I channeled the crystal, trying to recover my magic, but Sean was faster. His martial arts skills kicked in and he instantly engaged with the men, not giving me any chance to act.

I stared in awe. Had I thought Shade was Bruce Lee? No way, Sean was like him and Jean-Claude Van Damme and Jackie Chan and Jet Li all rolled into one. He moved as fluidly as water, as treacherous as a viper, and as strong as a bear. He kicked, dodged, twisted out of the way, punched, and blocked in a beautiful dance.

But then a third member joined the fight, and a fourth one came from behind, reaching for me.

With a yelp, I sidestepped him and threw my hand out. A small sizzle of magic sparked from my hand and into the man's chest. He quivered with the shock, but advanced with a murderous glint in his dark eyes.

Someone grabbed my wrist and twisted me around, and out of the way. Sean held my wrist as he landed a kick to the man's temple, knocking him out instantly.

He turned to me, his eyes wide. "Are you all right?"

Stunned, I nodded.

Footsteps and yells filled the place—more Brotherhood of Purity members were coming.

"Time to go!" Shade yelled from somewhere beside us. There were at least five men down around him, and he fought another two with ease. "Use the crystals!"

"Right." Sean fished small crystals from his pocket.

I frowned. "What is that?"

He showed me a sly grin. "Gifts from Khalisa."

He threw the crystals at the doorway we had emerged from. "Run!" he yelled, grabbing me once more and pulling me with him.

We ran to the entrance. Shade knocked a man down, and pushed the other back, then ran with us.

A second later, a boom echoed behind us and the walls shook.

Crystal bombs? That did sound like Khalisa.

We burst through the front doors into the dark night and continued running.

"I'll get the car," Shade said. A second later, he turned into the black cat and ran down the street.

I limped forward, my mind more confused by the minute. "The car?"

"We left a car hidden in an alley two blocks from here," Sean explained. He tugged at my hand, and I tripped on my own tired legs, but Sean only tightened his grip and brought me closer to him. "It's almost over. Hang on."

"Stop!" a voice came from behind us.

I dared glance over my shoulder. Maren and several Brotherhood members spilled from the front doors, rushing after us.

"Shit," Sean muttered. He wrapped an arm around my waist, half-carrying me as he ran down the street.

A second later, a black sedan turned a corner, the wheels squealing. It drifted to a stop a few feet from us.

"Get in!" Shade said from through the open window at the driver's door.

Sean opened the back door, pushed me in, then scooted beside me. "Go!" He closed the door as Shade stepped on the accelerator and the car lurched forward.

I looked back. Maren and the others had stopped the chase, but something inside me told me this wasn't over.

4

"Are you okay?"

I snapped my head to Sean. He was seated beside me, his hands hovering at my sides, his eyes tinged with worry.

I scooted as far away from him as I could get in the car. "Let me out." I looked at Shade. "Let me out right now."

Shade shook his head. "If I let you out now, the Brotherhood will have you again in less than five minutes."

"What about you? Aren't you members of the Brotherhood?"

Sean frowned. "Hazel, we just freed you."

"Are you working with someone else? Who is paying you?"

Shade scoffed, but said nothing, his eyes on the road as he zipped through the streets several miles above the speed limit.

"Hazel, it's not like that," Sean said.

"I saw you!" My voice rose and my blood boiled. The adrenaline of the run was fading, along with the power I had absorbed from the crystal. I could feel the exhaustion and the pain surging in every inch of my body. "You were with Maren and the others."

"I—"

"We're here," Shade said, interrupting Sean. Shade turned the car onto a street and I recognized it. We were outside Towland and stopping in front of Sean's building. Shade turned in the seat, looking at me. "Go with Sean. He will take care of you and explain his side of the story. When you're better, I'll explain mine."

I stared at them. They were nuts. I pushed the car door open and ran. In five seconds, I was panting and hurting and I knew I would faint.

Something jolted me and I blinked. "What—?" Sean carried me up the stairs. I pushed against him, but had no strength left.

"It's okay, Hazel," he said, his voice low, gentle. "You passed out for a minute." Holding tighter to me, he unlocked his apartment's door and walked inside. He kicked the door closed and deposited me on his bed. Then he took several steps back. "I know you don't trust me right now, but I promise you, I'll never hurt you. Right now, you need rest. Just ... lie down and rest. We'll talk when you're feeling better."

"I ..." I tried moving off the bed. I wanted to yell and run and disappear, but I couldn't.

The exhaustion and pain won, and I fainted again.

I DIDN'T HAVE A RESTFUL SLEEP. SEVERAL TIMES, I TOSSED and turned, and I thought I saw Sean sitting beside me. I remembered him placing a wet rag on my forehead, then later cleaning and bandaging the wounds around my wrists, and even helping me drink some water ... and medicine? But all the while, I was delirious with exhaustion.

Light filtered through the window, and I turned toward it. Sean was there, seated in a chair beside the bed, his torso folded over the mattress, a rag in his hand.

I watched him for a moment.

What the hell was happening here? He was a Brother-hood member, but had felt bad about imprisoning me, so he helped me escape? And now he was taking care of me?

One thing I was sure of, though: He didn't want to kill me. Otherwise, he would have already done so.

With a groan, I propped myself up, but before I could fluff the pillows at my back, Sean jerked awake.

"Wait, I'll do it." He seemed a little dazed while he reached around me and helped me with the pillows. He was so close, his arms inches from mine, his face even closer. "Better?"

Not trusting my voice, I nodded.

"I'll make us breakfast." He stood. "Why don't you get a shower and clean up? There's a change of clothes in there and a spare toothbrush." He frowned. "Do you need help?"

I shook my head. "No, I think I've got it."

He watched as I slid off the bed and wobbled toward the bathroom. "Are you sure?"

I waved him off and disappeared inside his bathroom. I

found a pair of leggings and one of my tees on the counter. Had he gone to my dorm and gotten those for me?

It didn't matter.

I glanced at the mirror and almost screamed. Holy shit, I looked like hell. My blond hair was glued to my scalp, my face was paler and thinner, my cheekbones sharper. I had probably lost weight from not eating. I felt like hell.

I stared at the closed door. Should I feel this relaxed in Sean's apartment? I mean, my instinct right now was half to go with it and half to flee. What if he was biding his time before he killed me?

But he had rescued me, hadn't he? He had cleaned up my wounds, bandaged them. He had made sure I was comfortable and taken care of. And right now, he was making me breakfast.

My stomach growled.

At this moment, I really needed a shower and to brush my teeth for twenty-four hours nonstop to feel clean again, then I would worry about fleeing or not.

Though I wanted to stay in the warm water for the entire day, I knew I shouldn't. Besides, I had been up a few minutes and I already felt my strength leaving me. It would take me a few days to recover.

I washed as thoroughly as I could, then brushed my teeth, got dressed, and returned to bed. I had sat back against the pillows, a small hand towel around the length of my hair so it wouldn't get everything wet, when Sean came back to his room.

He held a tray. There was a plate piled high with

waffles, a small bowl with syrup, a cup of coffee, and milk on the side.

After eating nothing for so many days, I felt like bawling at the sight and smell ... God, I could cry.

Sean set the tray on the bed beside me. "It's from a mix, but it's better than nothing." He sat back on the chair. "Later, we can order lunch from anywhere you want."

My throat closed; my eyes stung with unshed tears. "Why are you being so nice to me? I thought you hated me?"

He exhaled. "Hazel, I never hated you." He picked up the fork and placed it in my hand. "Eat and I'll explain everything."

My stomach had a pit the size of the French Quarter. I couldn't argue with that. I crossed my legs in front of me and set the tray over my lap. Then I dug in.

Man, the waffles ... even if they were from a mix. Right now, they were the best thing I had ever eaten. Though I could have inhaled them all in three seconds, I forced myself to go slow, take bite by bite and chew several times before swallowing. I didn't need to get sick from eating so fast.

"I'm waiting," I said between bites.

"Right." Sean ran a hand through his hair, and I realized it was longer than before. Just a little, but enough for me to notice. He also had scruff over his lower face, as if he had been too busy to bother to shave.

"I'll help you," I said when he didn't start. "How long have you been a member of the Brotherhood of Purity?"

Sean shook his head. "Let me start from the beginning." He leaned back in the chair. "I went to see Khalisa a couple of weeks ago."

Oh, I remembered that. "I know. She told me."

"She did?"

I nodded. "Yes, but she didn't tell me why. She said I would have to ask you."

"Well ..." He bit the inside of his cheek for a moment. "I wanted to ask her how I could contact the Lightgrove coven."

I frowned. "Why?"

"Because I wanted to find out how I could join the Light Order."

I froze in a half-swallow and coughed, stunned. "Wait." I inhaled deeply. "Why?" I asked.

"Because ... I knew you like this witchy thing. I knew you had been made for it. I know you'll do amazing, you'll impress Moira, and you'll ace this initiate program, and you'll become a full-fledged member of the Lightgrove coven. And they will be lucky to have you."

"And?" I pushed the tray to the other side, suddenly not hungry anymore.

"And I knew that if I wanted to be in your life, I had to follow you. The only way I could think to do it was to join the Light Order."

My breath caught. "But ... the other day. You broke up with me."

"Right." He grimaced. "It was part of my test."

"What?"

"I talked to the Lightgrove council and the Light Order," Sean continued. "I was given a test, much like you had one before joining their initiate program. I was to approach a Brotherhood of Purity member who recruited young men. I had to convince the guy I was a good fit, and I had a week to do it. I had to join them and find out something useful within two weeks. I was told the Brotherhood would be watching me, so I thought I had to break up with you and make it look real so the Brotherhood would never find out about you and use you to get to me."

"But they got me anyway." My voice broke.

"It wasn't because of me," he said. "I had been accepted into the Brotherhood and finally asked to join them. I had no idea the mission was you and that you would be there. The moment I saw you, all hurt and bloodied and plain pitiful, my blood boiled. It took every ounce of my will to remain calm and not attack them all right then."

"I thought you knew about me all the time, that you had brought them to me."

Sean shook his head. "No, I had no idea. Once I left there, I called the Light Order right away and told them about you. They confirmed you had been missing for a few days, which I also didn't know, but they told me to not engage. To just observe and keep them informed while they prepared something. I asked what they would do, but they didn't tell me." He groaned. "I couldn't wait. I wouldn't wait. Good thing Shade found me before I did something stupid."

"Right, Shade. The cat. Is there an explanation for that?"

"Shade came to me right after I talked to the Light

Order. He came as a cat, and he shifted right in front of me. He told me he's Arianna's familiar and—

"Wait." I raised a hand. "He's Arianna's familiar? The Arianna?" As in the founder of the Lightgrove coven? How was that possible? He had to be hundreds of years old ...

"Yes, that's what he told me. He saw you being kidnapped and—"

"He tried to help me," I said, remembering that night.

"Right. But he wasn't prepared. We came up with a plan. The crystal and the magic bombs were his idea. We stopped by Khalisa and got those from her. Thank goodness she had those ready."

I shook my head, confused with so much information. "That's crazy," I whispered.

Sean wanted to join the Light Order. He had infiltrated the Brotherhood as a test. He had broken up with me so the Brotherhood wouldn't know about me. And he had freed me with the help of Arianna's familiar?

That sounded absurd.

"So ... you want to join the Light Order?"

Sean fixed his eyes on mine. "I disobeyed the order to not engage. I'm sure I failed." He reached over, taking my hand in his. "But it was worth it. You're here now, unharmed. Shade warded this building, so you're safe here. The Brotherhood can't find you."

I didn't want to think about Shade or the Brotherhood right now.

"You want to join the Light Order for me?" I turned my hand in his and held his fingers tightly.

He nodded. "Hazel ... there's something I need to tell

you." He moved from the chair to the edge of the bed and cradled my hand in both of his. His eyes never left mine. "I love you, Hazel."

My breath caught.

"I know we barely know each other. I know it's fast." He pressed his hand above his heart. "But I know it in here. I feel as if I had been waiting for you for an eternity and I finally found you. If you let me, I'll hold on to you for the rest of my life and never let you go."

Tears brimmed in my eyes. "Really?"

He chuckled. "Does that mean you like it?"

"Of course, I do." I moved to his lap and wrapped my legs and arms around him. I cupped his handsome face. "I love you too, Sean."

I lowered my head to his, but he met me halfway. Sean's lips brushed mine, softly at first, but I had no patience for that. I pressed my mouth to his and he closed his lips around mine, kissing me deeply and slowly.

Sean wrapped an arm around my waist and swiftly moved us. He laid me down on his bed and eased himself over me.

"Is this okay?" he asked, his lips pressed against mine. "Does it hurt?"

"It'll hurt if you stop."

A smile stretched over his mouth before he deepened the kiss again. One of his hands slid down my side and clamped down on my hips. He pulled back and looked into my eyes. "I want you so bad, Hazel, you have no idea."

I tugged my heels into his ass and wrapped my arms

around his neck, trying to hold him closer again. "I think I do."

One corner of his lips curled up. "I'm serious." He leaned into me again but stopped halfway. "Maybe we shouldn't do this. You're hurt and tired and—"

"Sean!" I almost snapped. "If it hurts, I'll let you know. Right now, just kiss me, damn it."

With a half smile, Sean lowered himself back to me, taking me to paradise.

5

SEAN RAN HIS FINGERTIPS OVER MY ARM, DRAWING SHIVERS from me. After we made love, we snuggled in his bed, him propped up on the pillows and me leaning against him, my back to his bare chest.

I rested the back of my head on his shoulders, and if it weren't for his gentle touch on my skin, I would have dozed off already.

I turned my face toward him, rubbing my nose against his neck. His arms tightened around me, and he placed a kiss on my temple.

I sighed, feeling happy.

Even if it was for a moment, I was happy. I knew that once we moved, once we let the things outside this apartment reach us, this happiness would take a backseat, and I didn't want that to happen just yet.

"I think you will be a great Light Order warrior," I said, barely containing the feelings inside my chest.

This man, this gorgeous man, wanted to ditch his

human life to come follow my magical one. It was all for me because he loved me.

I loved him.

Sean sighed. "Would have been is the right term. After disobeying them, I'm not sure they will have me." He pressed his soft, warm lips to my shoulder. "I don't regret saving you, but I confess now I'm worried they won't let me join their ranks and I won't be able to be with you like that."

I held on to his arms around me. "They would be crazy to pass on. But if they do, then I'll quit too. We can both do whatever we want."

"Don't you want to be a witch?"

I frowned. "I do, but now that I know your feelings, all I want is to be with you, wherever you are."

"Ditto."

I lifted my head and Sean captured my mouth with his. His hands slid down my stomach, down to—

His phone rang from the nightstand and Sean stilled. With a groan, he reached for it and glanced at the screen. "It's the dojang. Shit. I had training this morning and with everything going on, I forgot."

I glanced at him, a little coy. "It's okay if you want to go."

He stared at me as if I were crazy. "I'm not leaving you."

A smile tugged at my lips. I liked hearing that. "That reminds me." He reached down, to something on the floor beside the bed, and when he straightened, he had my purse. "I was able to grab it before we broke you out."

Relaxing against him again, I took the purse in my

hands and looked inside. Everything was still in there: my wallet, my cosmetics bag, and my cell phone.

I picked it up. "It's dead."

"Here." Sean grabbed a long cable from his nightstand and handed it to me.

I plugged it into my phone, but it took a minute for it to come to life again. But when it did, it started beeping and didn't stop for a long time. Dozens of messages and missed calls and voicemails appeared on the screen.

"Holy shit." I could see several from Moira and some from Krissa, but the rest were from numbers I didn't recognize.

I scrolled down and choose a random voicemail.

"Hazel, it's Grace again," the council member's voice rang clear through the speakers. "We're worried about you. Where are you?"

I skipped to the next one.

"Hazel!" That was Moira. "What the hell is going on? If you don't come to class in fifteen minutes, I'll have you expelled from the program."

The next one was still from Moira. "All right, it has been hours. No one has heard from you. What's going on?"

The next one:

"Hey." It was Rodd. "You've been missing for two days already. Tell me you just gave up and went back to your hometown." Behind me, Sean tensed. "Shit, I know that's not true because I called your mother and she said you're not there."

"Oh, shit, my mom," I whispered as I paused the

message. I checked my phone and sure enough, there were a few calls and texts from her and Amanda.

I typed her a message:

> Hi, Mom. Sorry I haven't answered the phone. I've been busy with school and the initiate program. I'll call you soon, okay?

I inserted an emoji blowing a kiss-heart and hit send.

"Are you friends with Rodd?" Sean asked, his voice a little gruff.

Right, Sean probably had met Rodd when he asked to join the Light Order. "He's Moira's son, can you believe it? He knows she hates me and tries to play it cool."

I glanced at Sean. He didn't seem happy. I took advantage of that. "Why? What if I had told you he was my friend ... would you be jealous."

He grunted and puffed out his chest. "Why would I?"

I rolled to my side and rubbed my nose on his neck. "It's okay if you were jealous," I teased. I grazed my teeth on his skin and Sean groaned. "It's sexy even ... to a certain extent."

With a grunt, Sean hooked an arm around my waist and twisted us. Suddenly, I was lying underneath him, and his lips brushed against mine.

A meow came from the window. Though the blinds were half closed, we could see the form of a black cat outside. On the second floor?

How ...

Sean sighed. "That's Shade."

"Great timing."

He chuckled, placed a soft kiss on my cheek. "We have all the time in the world to enjoy ourselves."

True, but I was still not ready to get out of this bed.

Sean moved to the edge of the bed, taking me with him, and I had no choice but to get up. Grudgingly, I got dressed. The only good thing about this was the fact that I could stare at Sean as he got dressed too. The man was lean and ripped and every muscle in his body was apparent and hard. As he pulled his pants on, his back and core flexed, and as he put on his shirt, his biceps and triceps bulged.

I was in awe.

I knew he was watching me too. I had thought I would feel embarrassed about it, but now that his eyes skimmed my skin, shinning with desire, I liked it. It made me feel sexy, strong, empowered.

A knock came from the front door, and with a groan, Sean ripped his gaze from me and went to it.

After a quick glance at me to make sure I was dressed, Sean opened the door. As a human, Shade waltzed in the apartment as if he owned it. I stared at him, still stunned. This man was the black cat who had been following me.

And he proclaimed to be Arianna's familiar?

"Why?" The question flew out of my mouth before I could register it.

Sean closed the door and Shade frowned at me. "Why what?"

"Why have you been following me?"

"Ah, right." Shade pulled out one of the dining table's chairs and sat on it, his posture impeccable. With his dark slacks and shirt, and his superior demeanor, he seemed like a fish out of water. "We'll get to that."

Skeptical, I sat on the couch and Sean sat beside me.

"Then tell me everything," I said.

Shade tsked. "I'm not sure I can tell you everything, but I can tell you enough."

"What does that even mean?"

"Will you hear me out or not?"

I glanced at Sean, not really being able to imagine Sean agreeing to work with him.

Sean shook his head, and as if he could read my mind, he said, "I know. He's obnoxious, but I had no choice. No one else was willing to help me."

And that hurt. I knew I was a novice and had no true allegiance to the Lightgrove coven yet, but I thought they would have cared. I mean, wasn't that what they did? Help the innocent against the Brotherhood, dark witches, and other evil beings? I mattered to them less than an unknown human?

I exhaled and glanced at Shade. "All right, let's hear it. Why don't you start by telling us how Arianna's familiar is still alive?" It was rare for witches to have familiars, and those were linked to their witches' lives. If the witch died, the familiar died with her. Not to mention, how the hell could he turn into a human?

"Arianna put a spell on me so I wouldn't die when she did," he answered, sounding mildly bored. "Brita and Anna found me, and they put another spell on me so I could turn human at will. They also made me immortal. At least until Arianna comes back."

I blinked. Wow ... all right, crazy. "So ... you've been just waiting?"

"Yes and no." He shook his head. "I've been waiting for Arianna, yes, but I also have been searching for her ashes, grimoire, and necklace."

I frowned. "Don't you need those things to resurrect her?" It didn't make sense that he was waiting for her before he found the items.

"There might be another way," he said quickly before he went on, "but we need the items, regardless."

"And why did the Brotherhood think Hazel knew where they were?" Sean asked the next question on my mental list.

"We're not sure," Shade said.

I tilted my head. "We?"

"I've said too much already." Shade stood. "As much as I would love to chitchat, I have plenty to do."

I pushed to my feet. "I don't think we're done. I still have several questions."

"And unfortunately, I can't answer ninety percent of them." He looked around, wrinkling his nose. "I'll let you ask me one more question before I go, but I can't promise I'll answer."

I bit the inside of my cheek. "Why did you help Sean rescue me?"

Shade tsked. "That's one I can't answer yet. Just know this: You need to be careful. You should go back to the Light Castle. That is still the safest place for you, but do not tell anyone about me, and more importantly, do not trust anyone."

"The safest place for me?" I crossed my arms. "And why should I trust you?"

"I'm Arianna's familiar. If there's one person, or familiar, you can trust in this entire world, it is me." He glanced at Sean. "And him. You can trust him."

Sean's brows curled down. "How do you know? You barely know me."

One corner of Shade's lips curled up. "Right, I don't know you." He turned to the door.

"What is that supposed to mean?" Sean asked at Shade's retreating back.

"Right? Everything you say raises another four questions," I said.

Shade stopped by the door, hand on the knob. "I know and I promise everything will be answered in time. For now, just lie low, be careful, and do not—"

"Trust anyone." I sighed. "We heard you the first time."

"Good." He pulled the door open but paused again. "About Krissa ..."

I gasped. Oh, shit, I had forgotten all about Krissa. The Brotherhood had held a dagger to her throat in their attempt to get to me. I placed a hand over my stomach, expecting the worse. "What about her?"

"She's fine," Shade said. "Doesn't remember a thing."

I narrowed my eyes. "How?"

Shade offered me that superior lopsided grin. "I'll be in touch soon." He walked out and closed the door behind him.

Sean raced to the door and opened it. He looked

around the hallway before turning to me and pulling the door closed again. "He's gone."

"Great." I put my hands on my hips. "I don't think that was helpful at all."

Sean nodded. "It wasn't."

I paced the living room, my mind reeling.

The Brotherhood of Purity had captured me in front of Krissa, who thankfully wouldn't remember anything, and I had been held for almost a week. They thought I had some connection to Arianna's necklace, grimoire, and ashes. The black cat was really following me, and it wasn't just a cat—it was a familiar. And not just any familiar. It was Arianna's familiar. The Lightgrove coven and the Light Order had seemed worried about my disappearance, but according to Sean, they hadn't acted on it, not even when they knew where I was being kept.

Nothing about this made sense.

I stopped and turned to Sean. "What now?"

He shrugged. "I guess we should go back to the castle and talk to the council. I probably need to give them a report about what happened and wait to hear I failed."

"You haven't failed."

"You don't know that."

My brows knotted. He had freaking rescued me. If the Lightgrove coven and the Light Order let him go because of that, they were nuts.

I let out a sigh. "I guess you're right. Let's go to the castle."

6

BEFORE GOING TO THE LIGHT CASTLE, I STOPPED BY MY dorm. Shade had said Krissa wouldn't remember anything, but I had to make sure she was all right.

As I suspected, she wasn't in the dorm, but there was a note on my bed.

Are you coming back, or what?

Typical.

I sent her a quick text:

> Hey. I might drop out soon. Just don't throw my things away yet. I'll come pick them up when it's time.

She answered right away:

> Sounds good to me.

I bit on my lower lip.

> Are you okay?

> Sure. Why?

> Nothing. See you soon.

Apparently, she really didn't remember anything, otherwise she would have picked a fight with me, I was sure of it. But what had Shade done to her? Was he more powerful than other familiars because he was Arianna's?

I shook my head as Sean and I left my room, still not believing that story. If he was Arianna's familiar, he would have been dead for years now.

I was so lost in my thoughts, I almost ran into Andrea and Brittany as they exited their room. Sean had to yank my arm and pulled me to him so I wouldn't bump into them.

"Hey." Andrea smiled at me. "Are you okay?"

"We haven't seen you around lately," Brittany said. "Krissa said you have been gone a lot."

"Yeah, I've been dealing with some stuff," I told them. "But I'm fine. How have you two been?"

"We're good." Brittany showed me the empty reusable grocery bag in her hand. "We're going to buy popcorn and some beer, and then watch some horror movies." She glanced at Sean. "You two are invited."

"We can't," Sean said, his voice cold. It reminded me of when I first met him, and he wanted to keep me away from him. Gosh, that seemed like a decade ago, not just a handful of weeks. "We have an appointment."

"Right," I said, realizing that if I chose the witchy life and gave up on my human life, I wouldn't see them anymore. And I kind of liked the few times I had hung out with them. I frowned. "I'll call you guys when I'm back so we can do something."

"Awesome." Andrea waved at us, then Brittany did. The two of them turned and skipped down the hallway.

Sean and I stayed behind a few seconds.

"You lied to them." His voice was low, but still cold.

"I know." I sighed. Telling them I would be back later was wishful thinking. I knew I couldn't keep up with both lives, and I had already made up my mind about which one I wanted. Unless the Light Order didn't accept Sean, then we would rethink this whole thing.

But I had never had friends before and these two seemed like they could have been good ones.

I shook my head again, focusing on the path ahead of me. "We should get going."

Sean's hand tightened around mine and he led us out of the building.

ON THE WAY TO THE CASTLE, I SENT A MESSAGE TO MOIRA, and Sean contacted the Light Order. We let them know we were coming, and once we crossed the portal, they were right there: Moira, Rodd, and Fynn.

Moira's brows curled down as her eyes took me in, from head to toe and back. "I see you're okay." She stared at Sean. "And you disobeyed direct orders." She shook her head. "Follow me."

She took the lead. Sean and I followed her inside the castle, and Rodd and Fynn fell into step at the rear. Four Light Order members joined the procession as the doors closed behind us.

I tensed. What was this? It seemed like they were arresting us, not welcoming us back.

As if noticing my tension, Sean's thumb drew circles on my hand, his grip as firm as before.

Two Light Order members were positioned at the council room's entrance. They saw us approaching, and after Moira's nod, they pushed the doors open.

We walked into the large room with the ten white chairs that formed a wide circle. Five of the chairs were occupied by Queen Denise and the council members: Lenora, Grace, Amelia, and Clara.

They looked at us—at me—as if they were seeing a ghost.

Moira stopped at the edge of the circle, gesturing for us to walk forward. Still holding hands, Sean and I took the last few steps until we were in the center of the circle. Fynn and Rodd stayed behind with Moira.

I glanced at the queen and lowered my head.

"Are you all right, Hazel?" the kindness in her voice took me by surprise. She absently petted her red bird, who was perched at the arm of her chair.

I nodded. "I am now."

"We were so worried," Grace said. Her green snake coiled around her chair.

"What happened?" Lenora asked. Her owl perched along one of the white wooden beams adorning the high ceiling.

I frowned. Didn't they know already? "I thought Sean had called the Light Order."

Denise nodded. "He did, but we only knew that the Brotherhood of Purity captured you."

"And you told him not to do anything." I clamped my mouth, not believing I had said that to the queen. I lowered my head a little. "Forgive me."

"I understand your frustration and I'll explain our reasoning, but first, tell us what happened." It wasn't a question; it was an order.

I stood taller.

So, I told them everything. About going after Karl to find out about Doug, Sean's friend. About the Brotherhood of Purity finding me. About running away, getting to the dorm, only to find them there, with Krissa in their clutches.

"They took me," I continued. "I woke up two days later and was questioned about Arianna's grimoire, necklace, and ashes. For some reason, the Brotherhood seems to think I know where these items are."

The council members exchanged glances. Some had neutral expressions, but Lenora had huge eyes, and Clara had paled. What the hell?

"But you don't," Queen Denise said.

"Right, but they insisted." I told them about being without food and almost no water for three days, and then finally being found by Sean, who was there on a mission for the Light Order. "He told me he contacted you and you told him to stay put and not act."

Queen Denise nodded. "That is right." A stab to the heart. Ouch. It hurt to hear that. "But it isn't because you don't matter. Quite the opposite. We wanted to gather more intel before barging in and risking hurting you in the process."

My brows curled down. Was that true or was she saying that to make me feel better?

Queen Denise gestured to her son. Fynn stepped forward and spoke, "Sean, your test was to infiltrate the Brotherhood of Purity and find out what they were up to. You did that, however, you disobeyed direct orders and you blew your cover before fully understanding what they wanted with Hazel."

Beside me, Sean stilled. "Does that mean I failed?"

"I'll be honest, we're still debating that," Fynn said. "You did save Hazel and she's unharmed. That will be taken into consideration."

"So ... no answer yet?" I asked, a little worried.

Fynn shook his head. "The Light Order captains have a meeting scheduled for this evening to discuss this situation. We'll come to a decision and let you know."

I wanted to advocate for Sean, to come to this meeting and give my testimony, if necessary, but when Fynn retreated without another word and Queen Denise let out a heavy sigh, I knew I should keep my mouth shut.

"Hazel, because of recent events, I urge you to reconsider continuing your affairs in the human world," she said, her tone solemn. "Despite not having found your affinity and lacking knowledge about our history, Moira tells us you're dedicated and determined, two important traits in a powerful witch."

I stared at Moira, who looked straight ahead, ignoring me as usual. She said what? I needed to clean my ears. There was no way I had heard Queen Denise right.

"Dear Hazel, while you think this over, you should be careful when in New Orleans," Grace said, her eyes sympathetic and her voice gentle. "We don't want anything bad to happen to you."

"I'll do my best," I said.

"You should go," Queen Denise said. "Rest, eat, take tomorrow off. Monday, be ready to go back to your normal activities and resume your training."

I nodded, started to turn, but then stopped. "May I ask you something?"

"Of course," the queen said.

"Why do you think the Brotherhood thought I knew about Arianna's things? Did you know they are after the items? What they plan on doing with them?" Legend said that once the items were reunited, Arianna could be resurrected, but I doubted the Brotherhood wanted to bring back the founder of our coven, one of the most powerful witches in existence.

Queen Denise pressed her lips tight. "I don't know why they thought you knew. I had my suspicions that they were up to something that involved Arianna, but I had no idea what, and I can only hope they never find her items and we don't find out what evil things they plan on doing with those. Even if they don't use them to bring her back, her items are powerful. They could use them against us ... and that would be catastrophic."

I nodded, but still felt full of questions and doubts. "Thank you," I muttered.

From the sidelines, Moira urged me to come to her.

I nodded my head at the queen and the council members before following my mentor out of the room. Fynn and Rodd stayed behind, probably to talk to the council about Sean.

When the doors closed behind Sean and me, Moira turned her furious eyes to me. "You—"

The doors opened again, and Grace walked out. "Hazel, dear. I'll escort you to your bedroom."

7

Moira clamped her mouth and froze, as if she had suddenly become a popsicle. Grace just gave her one reassuring smile. "I'll take it from here," she said, her tone laced with a warning.

Moira hesitated, but after a glare at me, she whirled on her heels and marched away.

Grace turned her gaze, this time a little softer, to Sean. "Young man, you'll be escorted back to New Orleans." She gestured behind us.

We glanced over our shoulders and saw a member of the Light Order waiting for Sean a few steps back.

Sean looked at me, clearly uncomfortable with this. He held my hand briefly, gave it a little squeeze. "I'll call you later."

I nodded, a small smile on my lips. After another second, Sean let go of my hand and follow the warrior out of the castle.

I wanted to watch him until he disappeared from my

sight. No, I wanted to go after him and kiss him, and hold on to him forever. I didn't like seeing him walking away like that.

Grace cleared her throat, bringing my mind back to her. She beckoned me to follow her. She walked leisurely and in silence at first. But once we started up one of the wide, stone staircases of the castle, she finally glanced at me.

"I'm glad you're okay."

"You don't need to do this," I said quickly.

"Do what?"

"Accompany me to my room."

"Don't be silly, dear. I want to." She placed a hand to her chest. "I was worried when we realized you went missing."

I frowned. "How did you realize it?" I wanted to know what was going on while I was away.

"On Monday, you didn't show up for your meeting with Moira. After she was done with her morning lesson, she stormed into the council room screaming that you were reckless and that you should be expelled." Grace shook her head. "But I knew right then that something was wrong. I knew you wouldn't just disappear. I talked to the council members and the queen, and since you weren't answering your phone, we sent two members of the Light Order to New Orleans to search for you. They went to your dorm room, your classes, and even to the Midnight Cauldron, but no one had seen you, no one knew where you were."

"The Midnight Cauldron?"

She offered me a knowing smile. "You've been there a couple of times." True. And creepy. The Lightgrove coven seemed to know everything. "Anyway, we got together and dispatched a team to search for you. By then, we had our suspicions that the Brotherhood had taken you, but there was no confirmation until Sean contacted us yesterday." She leaned closer to me. "I'll tell you a secret. I wanted to get two dozen witches and a small Light Order battalion to go after you, but some council members thought it was too risky. The Brotherhood could kill you before we even found you."

True, but it still hurt. "So, what was the plan?" Just leave me there?

"We planned on sending Sean back to gather intel, numbers, protection spells, exits."

"But Sean didn't want to wait."

"No, he didn't." Grace smiled. "That young man really loves you."

My cheeks heated up. "I'm worried about him losing his place in the Light Order because of this."

She tsked. "Don't worry. I'll be there during the meeting, and I'll advocate for him. He was brave, and that must count for something, don't you think?"

We reached the hallway where my bedroom was located. Mei was walking out of her room. "Hazel! You're back!"

"Yes, I am."

She halted right in front of me. "Where were you? What happened?"

I glanced at Grace, confused. Hadn't they told the others I had been kidnapped?

"Hazel has been through quite the experience, dear," Grace said, taking the lead. "She needs to rest now. Tomorrow, she'll join you for class and she can tell you all about it." Grace waved at Mei to move along.

Flustered, Mei waved at me and walked away.

Grace and I arrived at my room's door. "Grace, if I could ask another question ..."

"Of course."

"Why would you rescue me? I'm just an initiate, and a not a powerful one at that." I had been wondering that. "I mean, not that I'm not grateful." I didn't want to die. "But ... I'm a nobody."

Grace grasped one of my hands and sandwiched it between both of hers. "My dear, every witch in this castle is valued. While in the initiate program, you are our responsibility. We wouldn't let anything happen to you."

But it had. And they had delayed coming to me. If it weren't for Sean and Shade, I would probably be dead now, probably from starvation.

I nodded. "Thanks. And thank you for walking me."

She pated my hand. "My pleasure." She gestured to my closed door. "Now go in and rest. Tomorrow is a brand-new day." She shooed me toward the door.

I opened it, stepped inside, and closed it, and all the while, Grace watched over me.

Queen Denise told me to take Sunday off to rest, but all it did was stress me out and make me restless. I hated being cooped up in my bedroom. After a visit from a healer witch who had been sent by the queen to make sure I was okay, I had gone to the library, walked around the garden, but even that didn't do anything to make my day more tolerable.

I considered going to New Orleans and spending the day with Sean, but the idea made me uneasy. I "should be careful." What did that mean exactly? I couldn't walk around the French Quarter alone anymore? I couldn't go to my dorm room? To classes?

I was becoming paranoid.

At least, it wasn't like I had nothing to do. Dear Moira had sent over books and texts and all the lessons I had missed this week with a nice note on top saying that if I didn't catch up, she would write a report about it.

She really did hate me.

In the evening, I gave in and joined the others for dinner. For the first time, I was the center of attention and I regretted coming.

"If you don't tell us what happened, we'll take turns guessing," Cleo said. She was seated to my right, Mei was on my left, and Belinda and Laini were on the other side of the table.

The other novices sat at the other tables spread through the hall, but they all kept glancing at our table. I guess me being gone for almost a week had been more noticeable than I thought.

Yesterday, Grace dismissed Mei when she asked about

it, giving me the impression that the council hadn't told anyone about my kidnapping. I wondered why. However, I didn't want to anger the council by running my mouth.

"There's nothing to tell," I said. "I was just … not here." I shoved a forkful of pasta in my mouth. I had been eating like crazy since being rescued from the Brotherhood, and I could only assume it was because they had starved me, the bastards.

Laini stared at me from under her fake lashes. "You're hiding something."

I shrugged. "Even if I am, you can't be sure."

"Grace walked her to her room yesterday," Mei said it as if that was a big deal.

"It's not the first time she has done that."

They all stared at me with huge eyes.

Belinda leaned forward. "You do realize a council member wouldn't be doting on a weak, non-legacy novice if there wasn't something special about her?"

I almost laughed and spit out the pasta in my mouth. I forced myself to calm down, chew, and swallow. "The only thing special about me is the fact that I'm eighteen and I still don't have an affinity." Which was pitiful, really. I hated being the outcast of this castle.

Laini narrowed her eyes. "No, there's more."

I rolled my eyes. "No, there isn't." Because if there was, I would know, right?

"Then tell us, where were you this past week?" Cleo asked, the amusement gone from her tone. They were losing their patience with me.

So was I. I stood and picked up my tray from the table. "You guys don't stop, do you?" I groaned and walked away. There was still one fourth of the pasta on my plate, but I didn't want to stay in this room for one more second. I put the tray away on the cleaning rack and stomped out of the mess hall.

I was so pissed, I almost rammed into Sadie as she turned the corner, an open book in her hands.

"Hey, I'm sorry." I stepped back.

"No, it was my fault." She pointed to the book. "I shouldn't walk and read at the same time." She looked fully at me. "Your aura ... you're mad. What happened?" I let out another groan. Her hand rested on my arm. "Hey, it's okay. You don't need to tell me."

I forced myself to exhale. "Sorry, it's just ... the other initiates in my group were grilling me about—" I clamped my mouth shut. I probably shouldn't talk about this to anyone.

Sadie glanced around. Then she leaned closer and lowered her voice. "About the past week? Fynn told me. After Sean told him about you, he started putting a team together to rescue you, but the council delayed it. He and Rodd were about to do it themselves when they heard Sean had done it." She showed me a sympathetic smile. "Dangerous, but romantic."

"It was, but now he's probably failed the test and won't be allowed to join."

"Nah. I probably shouldn't tell you this, but Fynn told me that even though he wasn't raised like most members of the Light Order, he hasn't seen a recruit with Sean's skills in a long time. I think that if Fynn has a say, Sean is in."

That was a wonderful thing to know. "Unfortunately, it doesn't depend solely on Fynn, does it?"

Sadie shook her head. "No, but I'm sure he'll do his best to advocate for him."

"Thanks.

Her eyes glanced around me. "Your aura seems better."

"Talking to you helped."

"Well, I'm going to the courtyard with a handful of books, and I plan on ordering some hot chocolate. Want to join me? Then we can keep talking."

I liked that idea. Especially the hot chocolate part. "I would love to."

8

SUNDAY NIGHT, MOIRA SENT ME A TEXT TO COME TO CLASS early.

Still groggy with sleep, I forced myself to get up half an hour earlier, get a quick shower, and get dressed. I slipped into the main hall, where I grabbed a to-go coffee and a blueberry muffin and went to our normal meeting place— an adjacent room to the library.

Moira was there, looking as harsh and impassive as ever in a dark suit and a tight ponytail.

"Morning." I took my usual seat and tried my best not to glower at her. "You wanted to see me?"

"Yes," she snapped. She walked toward me but halted about three feet from the table. "How are you?"

My eyebrows meet my hairline. "Why do you care? I thought that if I never came back, you would be happy."

She pressed her lips in a thin line. "Though it might be hard to believe, I care about my students."

I almost spat the coffee I had been sipping. "Great way of showing it."

"Hazel!" She raised her voice. Cleared her throat. Smoothed her hands over her blazer. "I couldn't care less about your perception. What I care about is showing up, doing the work. Being efficient, determined, and brave." She paused. "Last evening, we had our meeting about Sean and we read his report. It seems you were determined and brave, and you didn't break easily when the Brotherhood threatened you." She glanced at my wrists, where the shackle marks still marred my skin. They were a lot fainter now, but it would take them a while to fade away. "I'm ... proud of you."

I rubbed at my ear. "Wait, I think I didn't hear you right."

"Don't make me repeat myself!"

I suppressed a grin, but then focused on something else she said. "You were at the meeting yesterday. What was decided?"

She shook her head. "I don't know. The council members dismissed everyone from the room, but the Light Order leaders. They will make an announcement today."

I thrummed my fingers against the table, knowing I would spend the rest of the day wondering when exactly we would hear about it. I glanced at my phone. We still had fifteen minutes before the others started arriving. "Anything else you want to discuss?"

"Actually, yes." That took me by surprise. Moira sat at the corner of the long table. "I've been researching what

Almae told us ... about the magic wrapped around you that is preventing you from accessing your affinity."

Right. I had totally forgotten about that. "And?"

"All I found was a curse that suppresses magic, but slowly kills the host. You don't seem to be dying."

I frowned. "We should have told the council about this. Maybe they know what this is, or one of them is powerful enough to break it."

Moira's eyes rounded. "No, we cannot tell the council."

"Why not?"

"Just ... trust me on this. Give me more time. I'll find out exactly what is keeping you from using your magic, who cast that spell on you, and why." She pointed her long finger at me. "But do not mention this to anyone else."

Well, that didn't sit well with me. What was Moira afraid of? That the council would find out something she was trying to hide? That she was the one who kept my magic concealed so I would fail the program and leave?

I sighed and nodded. "Okay. I'll be quiet."

"Good." She turned her back to me as the sounds of footsteps and voices came our way. The others were arriving.

Moira greeted Laini, Cleo, Mei, and Belinda. She was slightly less harsh and unpleasant with them than she was with me, which made me think she was like that all the time, with everyone. I thought for a moment but couldn't remember one occasion where I had seen Moira inter-acting with others and being caustic.

But I was curious why didn't she want me to tell

anyone about my magic? It was so odd. There was also Shade, who didn't want people to know he had helped Sean rescue me. What was it with everyone and the secrecy?

Moira started our lesson, and I was still a little behind, despite studying all day yesterday.

I was into the lesson at first, but then my mind drifted to the fact that over a week ago, I was trying to find out where Doug's ghost was and how to free him when all this mess started. If the Brotherhood hadn't attacked me, I might have found something and Doug could have been free by now.

That made me a little sad. I had promised Sean I would find his friend and help him. I had been determined before, but now that we had made up and were stronger than ever, I really wanted to do it.

But how?

"... dark witches have been growing in numbers with alarming speed during the last two to three decades. The biggest dark witch coven, the Darkmist, has become even more selective, which means increasingly smaller covens are popping up. These smaller covens are created hastily, and—"

I didn't hear the rest of Moira's lecture because her words had reminded me of something. The dark witch from the night of my test on Friday the thirteenth. She had been one of the dark witches opening the veil between worlds and bringing ghosts to Earth. She probably knew what they wanted with so many ghosts, why Lizzie's and Doug's never crossed over.

As far as I knew, the dark witch was being held in the castle dungeon.

And if I could talk to her, I could find Doug.

9

OF COURSE, THE PLAN SEEMED A LOT EASIER IN MY MIND. AT lunchtime, I grabbed my food and sat by myself to think.

The truth was, I had no idea if the dark witch was still in the castle, or still alive, and I couldn't ask without raising suspicion.

Maybe—

My phone buzzed with a text from Sean.

> I was called to the castle. I'll be there in thirty.

I gasped. The verdict! We would find out what would happen to Sean. I ate my lunch, then raced to the portal line outside the castle. I paced in front of the fourteen portals, anxiously waiting for Sean.

Rodd appeared by my side.

"Waiting for your boyfriend?"

I skidded to a stop. Right. I had told him before that there was someone in my life, and I was sure he had known it was Sean the moment he reached out to join the Light Order.

I frowned. Had Rodd held that against him and voted against Sean?

"Yes," was all I said.

Rodd nodded. "He seems like a good guy. I good fighter, with a good head."

"Does that mean—?"

He shook his head. "I can't say anything."

I stared at him. "Will I be allowed to be with him when you tell him."

"Yes." Fynn's voice came from the castle's entrance. He walked toward us. "As long as you're there as a spectator and don't interfere."

I bit the inside of my cheek. Shit, being quiet and not interfering might not be in my genes, but I would do my best. Before I could make him an empty promise, one of the portals shimmered and Sean walked through.

He saw me and offered me a lopsided smile. My heart kicked up a notch. I hadn't seen him since Saturday, and that had felt way too long.

He walked to me, leaned over me, and brushed his lips over mine. "Hi."

I reached up and grabbed the side of his black hoodie. "Hi."

Sean closed his mouth around mine, but before the kiss could really begin, someone cleared their throat behind us. Sean took a full step to the side but clasped my hand in his.

We followed Fynn and Rodd to the council room. The

queen and the other council members were there, as were two older men, probably the captains within the Light Order.

"I think we're all here," Queen Denise announced from her seat. She gestured for Fynn. "Since you were responsible for Sean Flaherty's test, please."

Fynn nodded and stepped into the center of the circle of white chairs. He looked at Sean. "You came to us to enlist in the Light Order, and you were given a test. If you passed this test, we would welcome you for a four-month intense training program. After four months, you would be given another test and if you passed that, then you would join our ranks."

Apprehension brewed in me. So many ifs, would, could, should ... did that mean Sean failed? If he had, I would forever feel guilty.

Sean nodded. "I remember."

"Your test was to infiltrate the Brotherhood during one of their covert recruiting sessions," Fynn went on. "And find out something valuable to us in a period of two weeks. However, in less than five days with them, you found out Hazel had been captured. You contacted us, we told you to stay put while we worked on a plan, but you disobeyed direct orders and rescued Hazel. You blew your cover and didn't find out anything we can use against them."

Sean lowered his head. "That's true."

"However, we realize that if you'd followed our orders, the Brotherhood would have either starved Hazel to death or killed her. You followed your gut and it paid off. We value that."

"What are you saying?"

"You passed the test." A smile broke out on Fynn's face. "You start training next week."

I gasped and Sean stared at me, his eyes wide. I screeched and hugged him. "Congratulations," I whispered.

His arms tightened around me. "Thank you."

"Be aware," Fynn continued. Sean and I pulled back but remained hand in hand. "The training will be hard. You'll have a room in the Light Order wing, and you'll be expected to follow all our rules and apply yourself. If you disobey us again ..."

"I understand," Sean said. "Thank you for this opportunity."

Fynn stepped forward and clasped Sean's forearm. "Believe me, our ranks are small and we welcome every capable and motivated male to join us. I'm rooting for you."

"Thanks," Sean said again.

"Thank you," I said too.

We turned to the queen and the council and uttered our thanks as they congratulated Sean.

The queen rose from her seat. "Sean Flaherty, I hope you know what an honor it is to join our ranks, and you keep the why you're joining close to your heart. Every witch in this castle, initiate or not, is valuable and cared for."

"I understand," he said, tense.

"You may continue with your human activities until your training is done, if you can keep up with both," she said. "If your training begins lacking, you will either have to abandon your human life earlier, or you'll be asked to quit."

"I ..." Sean opened and closed his mouth. "I'm not sure I'll continue with my human activities."

I glanced at him, not expecting that.

"Good." The queen nodded. "I expect to hear good things from both of you." She shifted her gaze to me, and I stilled.

Oh-kay.

With that, we were dismissed, and Fynn and Rodd escorted us out of the room. Once the doors closed behind us, Fynn and Rodd turned to us and congratulated Sean once more.

"Hazel, would you like to give Sean a tour of the castle?" Fynn asked.

"Of course." I loved that idea. I tugged Sean's hand. "Come with me."

Together, I walked with Sean through the castle. I showed him the mess hall, the library, the classrooms, the courtyard, the Light Order training ground, the Light Order wing, the side of the castle where the official Light Witches lived, and where the initiates slept.

I didn't think I was supposed to take Sean into my bedroom, but I couldn't help it.

I opened my arms and whirled around my room. "And here is where I am when I'm texting you late at night saying I'm bored."

He halted in front of the closed door, his eyes on me. I lowered my arms. "What?"

His lopsided grin was back. "I'm in."

I smiled at him. "You're in."

"We're in." He took a couple steps toward me.

"Well, technically, both of us still have to pass the probation period, but yes, I guess we are." I frowned. "Sean ... you're not sure you'll continue with Towland? And martial arts?"

He took another two steps and stopped right in my personal space, inches from me. "You're more important than anyone and everything else."

Oh, my heart ...

One arm wrapped around my waist, pulling me to him, and the other cradled my nape, as Sean lowered himself and claimed my mouth with his.

I hadn't expected to show him my bed, but I couldn't deny that was the best part of this entire visit.

10

With Sean coming to the castle and everything that happened after that, I had forgotten about my plan to find Doug and free his ghost.

I tried finding Rodd before class on Tuesday, but I had no such luck. As it was, I had class with his mother and the other girls, but my mind wasn't on it. All I could think of was my plan, and about Sean and the fact that he would be moving to the castle next week!

I wanted to go to New Orleans with him last evening, to help him pack, but he had stopped me at the portals. "No, Hazel, remember what Shade said. You should be careful, and roaming around New Orleans is the opposite."

I hated to admit it, but he was right.

So, I stayed, curled up in bed, and texted with him while he packed. He worried about the lease on his apartment, which ended next summer, but he was sure he could find someone to sublet it in the meantime.

During class, Moira was as pleasant as usual, and

talked about dark witches and when they interfered in human affairs for their own gain. Most of them I knew, but some were a surprise. The sinking of Titanic? The flu of 1915? The great depression? The black plague?

It was sickening.

Once we were dismissed for lunch, I ran out of the room before Moira could ask me to stay. She loved giving me extra work, or pointing out how far behind or unqualified I was to be a full-fledged Lightgrove witch.

I didn't know Rodd's schedule, but after asking around, I found him patrolling the corridor outside the library. I guess even high-ranked Light order members had to do tedious work every now and then.

He saw me and his march became a soft walk. "Going to the library?"

I shook my head. "Actually, I was looking for you."

He frowned. "Why?"

"Because I need your help."

"With?"

"Well ..." I glanced side to side, making sure we were the only ones in this corridor. "The dark witch I fought against during my test, is she still in the castle?"

"Why do you want to know?"

I almost grunted. Did he always have to answer with a question. "Answer me and then I'll tell you."

He considered that for a second. "Yes. She's in the dungeons underneath the castle."

"What's her name?

His brows curled down further. "Starla. Why?"

"I need to talk to her."

"Why?"

"Because she might have information I need."

"About?"

Again with the one-word questions. "Ghosts. I believe one of the ghosts she took was Sean's best friend, Doug. After the test, I promised to find Doug, but I have no leads. Except this dark witch. I need to—"

"No." He raised a hand. "Don't ask to see her. I can't take you there."

"Why not?"

"Even if I was willing to help you, which I'm not, I can't. She's under heavy security and only captains have access to her."

"Shit." I had thought that because Rodd had seemed to care for me before, he would be willing to help me. But Fynn? I barely knew him. He would never help me.

Sadie turned a corner on the corridor, a book in hand, and her eyes narrowed. "Your auras ... what are you two hiding?"

"Nothing," we both said in unison.

She walked up to us. "And now I want to know even more."

I hesitated but decided to tell her. After all, she was Fynn's girlfriend. I told her about the dark witch, Doug's ghost, and my promise to Sean.

"If all you need to do is talk with the witch, it shouldn't be too hard," she said. "Rodd doesn't have clearance, but Fynn is there all the time." She picked up her phone. "What's your phone number? I'll talk to Fynn and text you."

I smiled. "That's great, thanks."

"Don't thank me just yet. We'll see if I can convince Mr. Do-It-All-Right to help us."

My chest constricted a little. She said us, as if she were a good friend and my problems were hers. I liked that.

She waved at me and disappeared into the library.

I stood there, amazed that my plan would work. "Thanks," I said to Rodd.

"I didn't do anything."

"No, but you listened, and you didn't tell your mother I want to see the dark witch."

One of his brows lifted. "I still might."

I knew he was teasing me. "I won't hold it against you."

"I have to resume my patrol." He took two steps back. "See you later, Hazel."

With a sigh, I headed to the mess hall to grab a quick lunch. I had another class with Moira this afternoon, and I wasn't looking forward to that.

However, my entire day brightened when I got a text from Sadie about an hour later.

> I've talked to Fynn. He's in. Meet me outside the hall at 11.

I FELT LIKE I WAS ROBBING THE CROWN JEWELS. AFTER dinner, I went to the library and tried to study while waiting for the right time. Not knowing what Sadie's plan was, I dressed in black leggings, a thin black sweater, and my soft black boots, so I wouldn't squeak on the castle's stone floors.

Three minutes to eleven, I made my way out of the library, forcefully yawning. If a Light Order guard saw me, he would think I was heading to my bedroom. I dashed to the mess hall as fast as I could without making much noise and being careful not to run into a patrol. I slowed down at the hall's main entrance, looking around.

Where was Sadie?

"Hey."

I jumped and slapped a hand over my mouth before the shriek in my throat burst out. "Holy shit." I glared at Sadie. She had come out of the dark hall, scaring the shit out of me.

"Sorry." She smiled at me. "Ready?"

I frowned. "What are we doing?"

"Fynn is on duty tonight. He signed up Rodd to replace the other guard, and they will let us in."

"That simple?"

She shrugged. "That's good, right?"

I nodded. Right. I shouldn't be so suspicious. I hoped more things in my life were simple and easy.

Together, we turned down a long and wide hallway. After a few steps, the hallway narrowed. A thick, white door stood at the end of the corridor.

Fynn and Rodd stood guard.

Without a word, Fynn unlocked the heavy door and pulled it open for me.

"She's the only one down there," he said. "Just remember everything in there is enchanted. Do not touch anything with your bare skin. Not the bars, the floors, or the walls."

I nodded, worried about breathing in there. "I'm going in alone?"

"We have to stay here," Rodd said.

Sadie touched my arm. "I can go with you, if you want."

She didn't really seem to think that was a great idea. "No, it's okay. If she can't cast any spells or leave her cell, it should be fine."

"It will be fine," Fynn assured me.

I inhaled and walked past the door.

They closed the door behind me with a definite thud, and I almost jumped out of my skin. Holy shit. I blinked in the darkness for two seconds, until my eyes adjusted and I finally saw the doorway across the small space, and the faint lights hanging from the ceiling.

The doorway led to dark stairs. From here, I couldn't see their end. All right, Hazel, time to woman up! I braced myself and trudged down the stairs. I tried not counting each step as I went down and down and down, deep into the earth underneath the castle.

I had to take several long breaths and remind myself this was fine. This place had been built centuries ago, was reinforced with magic, and there was nothing that could make the walls cave in on top of me.

Right?

Finally, the stairs ended in a curved archway. I walked by it and felt an energy rush through me—a spell. The archway was enchanted. Probably to keep the prisoners in.

I shuddered and focused on the long, wide corridor in front of me.

Like the stairs, faint lights hung from the ceiling, illuminating the bars lining the sides and the occasional stone pillar, separating the cells. It was easy to spot where the dark witch was. Her cell was the only one with dark glowing bars—another spell. I sucked in a deep breath and walked to it. I stopped right in front of the cell.

The witch reminded me of how I had been not a handful of days ago, at the Brotherhood's hideout: seated in the center of an intricate white witch's circle and wrists bound, though her shackles shone like the bars.

She sat with her legs crossed in front of herself, her hands between her legs, her head drooped forward, and her long dark hair acting as a curtain.

She didn't look intimidating or powerful with her dirty hair, ragged clothes, and wispy figure. Were they feeding her, or letting her starve like the Brotherhood did with me? I understood she was a dark witch, but we weren't like our enemies, were we?

Still, something clenched in my stomach when she moved her head up and spied me from under her hair. "It isn't polite to stare," she said, her voice parched.

I straightened my back, lifting my chin. "Do you remember me?"

A low laugh echoed through her cell. "The weak witch who put me in here?" Technically, I hadn't put her in here. I had defeated her, and then the Light Order had taken her away. "How could I ever forget you?"

I frowned, reminding myself she couldn't do anything

while behind those bars. "Good," I said with a smack of my lips. "I need to ask you a question and—"

Another low laugh. "Who says I will answer it?"

I knew that was a possibility. "What were you doing with the ghosts? Why did you need them?"

The witch tilted her head and her hair parted, revealing a little more of her face—gaunt, pale, bony. Seriously, I had to talk to someone. Weren't they feeding her? She may be a prisoner, but we had to show decency.

I was sure the others wouldn't agree with me, though.

Her dark eyes locked on me, her gaze so intense, it was as if she could see my soul. "Use your imagination."

Uncomfortable with her stare, I shifted my weight. "I bet the answer is different from whatever I could come up with."

"True." The witch nodded once. "But I still won't tell you."

I took a step closer, feeling the heat of the spell on the bars. "Starla, please. Just ... tell me where to find them. I need to find one of—"

Her cackled resonated through the entire dungeon. The hairs on my arm stood on end. "Stupid, weak witch. You're wasting your time. I didn't tell those puny warriors anything, and I won't tell anything to the likes of you."

I pressed my mouth into a thin line. Damn it. "What do you want?"

She narrowed her eyes. "Freedom. Can you give that to me."

I stayed quiet.

She tsked. "I thought so. Now stop bothering me and go."

I clenched my hands into fists. The audacity. She was the one behind bars! But she wouldn't answer any of my questions, no matter how many times I asked or begged. This was a big waste of time.

With my tail between my legs, I retreated from her cell and climbed the dark stairs.

Sadie was outside the door, waiting for me. Fynn and Rodd were right beside her. "How was it?" she asked, sounding like she really cared. She took a good look around me. "You're sad. She didn't tell you anything."

I sighed. "No, she didn't. I expected as much, but ..."

"You had to try," Rodd finished for me.

I nodded.

Sadie placed a gentle hand on my arm. "I'm sorry."

"It's okay," I mumbled. "I need to find another way to find out where the ghosts are."

"If you need our help, let us know." She glanced at the guys. "Right?"

"Right," Fynn said right away.

It took him five seconds, but Rodd nodded.

"Thanks," I said, sounding and feeling defeat. "Right now, I want my bed."

Sadie hooked her arm around mine. "Let's go together." She waved at the guys. "Good night."

"Night," Fynn and Rodd said in unison.

As we were leaving, I glanced over my shoulder. "Thank you again for helping me."

Rodd's eyes softened. "Of course."

11

I GRABBED A BIG PLATE OF WAFFLES AND SYRUP, PUT IT ON MY tray, and headed to my usual table with the other witches in my initiate group. Before I could sit with them, Sadie waved me over. She was seated with Fynn and Rodd at a smaller round table to the side.

I hesitated. Per the rules, I had to sit down with my group, but I didn't really like those girls, while Sadie, Fynn, and Rodd had been nothing but kind to me.

And after last night, I felt like we had a secret group of our own.

"Morning," I said, taking my place between Sadie and Rodd. I glanced at the guys. "Did you sleep?"

Fynn shook his head. "No. We just finished our shift. We're going to bed after we eat."

My stomach clenched. This was because of me. "Sorry I made you stay up all night. For nothing."

"It's okay," Rodd said. "Every now and then, we need to work the graveyard shift." He bit his bacon.

"So, what now?" Sadie asked. She had already finished eating her breakfast. The guys were almost done, and I had barely started.

I swallowed a big bite of waffles. "I don't know. I was following another lead when the Brotherhood found me ..." I shoved another piece of waffle in my mouth.

"But that means you know where to look? The dark witch isn't your only lead?"

I shook my head. "No, she isn't. But I'm not so sure about trying to find the ghosts again. What if the Brotherhood is waiting for me?" Because they had been waiting for me. If not waiting, then hunting me, a weak witch who couldn't even find her own affinity.

"Then we go with you," Sadie said. She glanced at the guys. "Right?"

"Can we sleep first?" Fynn asked. "If there's a chance we'll run into the Brotherhood, Rodd and I need some sleep."

Rodd nodded.

I held my breath. "You guys don't need to." They owed me nothing. I didn't want to be indebted to them.

"We want to." Sadie sounded mildly excited. "That's what friends do. We can go later this afternoon, after the guys have slept."

Friends.

Sadie, Fynn, and Rodd were my friends.

Oh, shit ... Rodd's mother.

"Hm, I might have a meeting with Moira then, and if she finds out what I'm up to ..."

"Don't worry about her," Rodd said. "I'll tell her you

are helping with Light Order business. She won't be able to say anything."

"I don't want to put you in a bad spot with your mother."

Rodd shrugged. "Nothing new."

My brow furrowed. "You get in trouble with your mother?"

Fynn snorted. "All the time."

I sighed in relief. "Sorry but I must confess that's good to hear. I thought she only disliked me."

"Oh, no, she dislikes everyone," Rodd assured me. "But you above everyone else."

I TOLD SEAN OF OUR PLAN, AND HE WAS WAITING FOR US outside the antique store in the French Quarter. When he saw Fynn and Rodd, he stood taller, and greeted them respectfully.

"Relax, soldier," Fynn teased. "We're off duty now."

Sean relaxed a smidge. He grabbed my hand, entwined his fingers with mine, and only placed a soft kiss on my cheek. Was he afraid Fynn or Rodd would fail him because he kissed me? I mean, wasn't I the reason he was joining the Light Order in the first place? He better kiss me!

I grabbed the collar of his hoodie and pulled him to me. I pressed my lips to his and thankfully, he didn't fight me on this. Not for even half a second. Quite the opposite. The moment my lips touched his, he closed his mouth around mine and kissed me.

But we had an audience, and we were in the middle of a busy street, so I broke the kiss and whispered, "Better."

His perfect lopsided grin adorned his lips.

The hotel was a handful of blocks from the antique store, so we walked toward it, blending in with the tourists. It was late afternoon, and it was still warm out.

Even though it was a Wednesday, this place would be even more crowded soon, but the alleys around the hotel would be darker.

When we got to Hotel Monteleone, I directed them to the alley I had seen Karl in, but paused at the entrance. Last time I was here, the Brotherhood attacked me, and I ended up in their prison for several days.

"It's okay," Sean told me, his voice low. His hand squeezed mine. "We are here and won't let anything happen to you."

I inhaled deeply and nodded. I was stronger than this. With decisive steps, I marched into the alley.

"There are several ghosts around this area." I let go of Sean's hand, opened my tote, and picked up my white chalk.

"I don't think we need that." Sadie offered me her hand. "We should be able to summon him if we join our magics."

That would certainly be easier. I took her hand in mine, and while thinking of Karl, I whispered, "*Apparet.*" Beside me, Sadie didn't say anything, but I could feel her magic swirling around the alley. She was powerful, and I was mildly impressed she didn't need to recite any words to make it happen.

The air shimmered in the middle of the alley, and it morphed into the shape of a person. I recognized him instantly. "Karl."

His ghost-white face didn't hide his surprise. "You again? I thought you were dead."

"I came to finish what we started."

He glanced to Sadie, Sean, Fynn, and Rodd. "What about the rest of you?"

"We're here to help her catch the dark witches who did this to you," Sadie said, her voice gentle.

Karl shook his head. "I don't think this is a good idea."

"Just tell us where to find the witches and the other ghosts; that's all we need to know." I paused. "Then I'll do what I promised you. I'll free you."

He hesitated, glancing at my friends again. Then he let out a long breath. "All right, I haven't been there in a long time, but last time I saw a handful of witches and an army of ghosts was at an abandoned shopping strip, Kingsley Center."

Fynn frowned. "I know where that is."

"That's the only place you remember?" I asked.

Karl nodded. "Other than that, I've been here since I died."

I let go of Sadie's hand and grabbed the pouch with the red powder from inside my tote. I threw a little of the powder over Karl's ghost and said, "*Liberi.*"

He exploded in white smoke.

I turned to the rest of the group. "We're going to the Kingsley Center, right?"

Everyone looked to Fynn. His brows knotted, but he nodded. "Let's go."

I HAD NO IDEA THE LIGHTGROVE AND THE LIGHT ORDER HAD a garage behind the antique store with all sorts of cars and equipment. The Light Order soldier pretending to be a janitor didn't even blink when Fynn walked in, greeted him casually, and then left driving a medium-sized silver SUV.

Fynn drove, Sadie sat in the passenger seat, and I was between Sean and Rodd in the backseat. Sean had a possessive arm around my shoulders, keeping me more to his side than Rodd's.

I almost rolled my eyes.

I had mentioned Sean to Rodd, but I hadn't mentioned Rodd to Sean, right? I mean, there was nothing to say, really, but I think that if for some reason Sean were to find out Rodd had danced with me at that ball and asked me out on another occasion, he wouldn't like it. I put myself in his shoes and thought I wouldn't like it either, so I made a mental note to tell Sean about it later.

Fynn slowed the SUV when we approached the abandoned shopping center. He drove by once, then he made a U-turn, parked the SUV half a block away, and turned off the lights. From here, we could see half of the place, but since it was getting dark, it was all a big gray building in the distance.

"What do you see?" Fynn asked Sadie.

"Nothing," she said. "Unless the witches can hide their auras, there's no one in there."

"Or this could be the wrong place," Rodd said.

"Or a trap," Sean added.

Karl wouldn't do that, would he? What would he gain? What could the witches have promised him? Freedom? That was what I gave him, not them.

"It's not a trap." I pushed Sean to the side. He got the hint, opened the car door, and we spilled out.

The others followed our lead.

We stalked in the shadows toward the abandoned strip mall, keeping close to the buildings—an office building, an open and empty parking lot, a small neighborhood grocery store with only two cars, and a diner with only one customer inside. If people took a closer look, they would think we were ready to rob a bank, dressed in black and tiptoeing our way through the dark—it was odd seeing the guys in black. They usually wore white, beige, or silver.

At the corner of the strip mall, Fynn asked Sadie again. "Any auras?"

She shook her head. "Nothing."

"Isn't that odd?" Sean asked. "Would the witches leave the ghosts by themselves?"

"Most ghosts can't wander off," Sadie said. "They are tethered to a place or a person. And I bet that the witches keep a ward or something around the building so they can't get away."

I inhaled. "And wards so others don't get in."

"Probably," Fynn said.

We inched toward the main store of the strip mall, a

place that could have easily been a Target or a Walmart. The sliding glass doors were covered with cardboard and the few windows on the building's side didn't show any lights coming from inside.

Fynn and Rodd took the lead and walked up to the doors. They didn't open. Fynn unsheathed his sword and wedged it between the doors. He was able to open them about two feet, enough for us to squeeze inside.

We glanced at each other as if daring who would go first.

Rodd grunted and stepped past the doors.

We quietly followed.

At first, I didn't see anything as it was too dark. Then my eyes adjusted to the darkness, as if by magic, dim light points shone from what seemed miles away. The place was one giant room with a few leftover shelves, and cash register counters, but nothing else.

At least, until we reached halfway.

We heard pained moans and mumbles, and it reminded me of movies when they depicted people in asylum.

"Who's there?" Fynn asked, his voice echoing through the giant room.

More mumbles and moans.

Then, a cold breeze blew from above and I knew ... "Oh, shit," I muttered as I looked up. Everyone followed my lead.

Dozens of ghosts roamed the top half of the room, like catatonic mummies. They seemed out of it, here but also not.

"Hello?" Sadie called.

No answer, just more moaning.

Sean started walking around, his gaze above his head. Looking for Doug.

Though I had only seen one picture of Doug on Khalisa's newspaper, I did the same.

"Why are all these ghosts here?" Fynn asked.

"I don't know," Sadie said. "What would the dark witches want with so many ghosts?"

"Can they absorb their powers?" Rodd asked.

"Ghosts don't have powers," Fynn observed.

"Right, but what else could it be? These are dark witches. All they want is power."

My attention was on the ghosts floating around the room. I saw so many of them—men, women, teenagers, young children, elderly. There was no discrimination here. The witches trapped who they could catch.

But why?

Looking up, I almost bumped into the wall. No, not a wall. I shifted my gaze and saw a long table along one of the walls. I took a few steps back. Shelves and other furniture crowded the table. Glass vials with dark iridescent liquid were on the table and on the shelves. I didn't know how I hadn't seen them from afar as they practically shone in the dark.

Hands trembling, I reached for one of the vials.

"Don't touch those!" Sadie appeared at my side and snatched my hand away. "We don't know what they are. It could be poison."

Rodd produced a handkerchief from one of his pockets. "Here." He gently wrapped the cloth around one of the vials and picked it up. "We should take it, see what it does."

"I found him!" Sean's yell came from across the room.

We raced toward him.

Sean pointed up to a thin ghost with unseeing eyes. If I hadn't seen his picture in Khalisa's records, I wouldn't have known this was the man I was looking for.

I placed a hand on Sean's shoulder.

"Hi, Doug," I said, relieved and saddened at meeting my boyfriend's best friend.

"Doug?" Sean asked. "Hey, Doug. Can you hear me?"

Doug kept floating slowly, his eyes unseeing. And to think that this could have happened with Lizzie, Sean's sister. Thankfully, she was able to get away before the dark witch had trapped her, and I had freed her weeks ago.

It was time to free Doug.

I fished the pouch with the hawthorn berry powder from my tote.

"Wait." Sean raised a hand. "Let me try talking to him first. I need to apologize—"

"I don't think he can hear you," Sadie said. "I don't think any of them can. Whatever the witches did to them, they aren't truly here."

Sean sighed. "I know. But ... I must try."

"We'll give you a minute, if you need it," I said.

Sean looked up at Doug again. A moment later, he shook his head, his eyes pained, and said, "It's okay. I want him at peace."

I looked down at the pouch in my hand. "I'm not sure I have enough for all the ghosts."

Sadie offered me her hand. "Use my magic. It'll increase the hawthorn berry powder's power and should do the trick."

I nodded. Sadie placed her hand on my shoulder, and slowly, we went around the room, throwing the powder at the ghosts and saying, "*Liberi*," repeatedly.

Until they were all gone. At peace.

Including Doug.

Fynn looked around. "It's done. And we have the vial. We should go before the witches come back."

We ran out of the building.

"ARE YOU OKAY?" I ASKED SEAN.

He leaned against the window, holding my hand in his. The lights from the street gave him dark shadows that enhanced the sharp angles of his face.

"I will be." He brought my hand to his lips, kissing my knuckles. "Thank you. For not giving up and giving me this closure."

"My pleasure."

Unfortunately, Sean couldn't go to the castle with us yet, so Fynn drove to his apartment first. I wanted to stay with him, but thought it was better if I went back to the castle. After all, the Brotherhood could still be after me and the last thing I wanted was for them to find me in Sean's apartment.

We rode to the French Quarter, dropped the SUV at the Lightgrove's garage and storage, and walked through the portal inside the antique store.

Before we reached the castle's door, though, Fynn turned to us. "Rodd and I will report this."

I froze. "What?"

"Don't worry, we won't tell them everything. We'll just say we stumbled on that place."

Rodd fished the wrapped vial from his pocket. "Otherwise, how will we explain this?"

"Right," I mumbled. I really hoped they spun this in a convincing way so the council didn't think I was out searching for more dangerous adventures and putting myself in trouble.

"Come on." Sadie grabbed my elbow and guided me into the castle. "Let's see if they are still serving dinner. I'm starving."

12

MOIRA WALKED AROUND OUR DESKS, CHECKING OUR grimoires over our shoulders. We were supposed to write a spell to counteract a small jinx curse, but I couldn't focus.

Since last night, all I thought about was the dark witch, Doug, and the other ghosts. I had freed Doug and should feel like I had closed this chapter, shouldn't I? Then why did I think there was so much more to this story? It didn't feel right. It couldn't be right. I wished the council would act.

These dark witches had to be stopped.

"Hazel Rose Levine?" a voice echoed through the library.

I snapped to attention.

Lenora stood at the library's entrance, her eyes on me.

Shit, this couldn't be good.

I stood. "Yes?"

"The council is calling for you."

I glanced at Moira, who shrugged and continued her stroll. My hands shook as I closed my grimoire and gathered my pens.

Whispers reached my ears.

"... think she'll be expelled?"

"... might have done something else wrong."

"... missing for an entire week."

"... always in trouble."

"... will let her go."

"... doesn't deserve to be here."

I pretended I didn't hear the others while I packed my things and hurried out of the library, following Lenora. What hurt the most was that Moira didn't stop the whispers. If I heard them, she did too, and even though she didn't like me, as an authority figure, she should have done something, right? Even if it was to tell them all to be quiet.

It didn't matter. I didn't need Moira's help. Their words didn't affect me in the slightest.

At least, that was what I told myself.

Lenora was quiet as she led me toward the council room. Her owl flew from doorway to doorway, always pausing wherever it could perch to wait for its witch.

I wanted to ask what this was about but I held my tongue. Knowing beforehand would only make my anxiety worse.

By the time we reached the council room, my hands were sweaty and shaking. Lenora gestured for me to drop my stuff in one of the empty chairs and I did so.

Queen Denise was the first to speak. "Do you know why you're here?"

"No, Your Majesty," was all I could muster.

"Early this morning, we received a report from my son, Fynn Lockwood, about last night's events. We know there's more to the report and we wanted to ask you what isn't being told to us."

My stomach dropped. Oh, they knew this was on me. Shit. I could keep lying but what good would that do? If they decided I was lying, I would be kicked out of the initiate program ... and I didn't want that, not anymore.

I wanted to be a full-fledged light witch in the Lightgrove coven. I wanted Sean to make it into the Light Order, and I wanted us to have a life together here in the castle, fighting evil, helping innocent witches and supernaturals, and growing old together.

I lifted my chin. "It's all my fault." I told them everything. Well, almost. I didn't tell them I had roped Fynn and Rodd to let me see the dark witch in the dungeons—that alone would be grounds for expulsion. But I told them the rest ... the first test, Sean's sister and best friend having died in that house. My promise to Sean. That I was investigating Doug's death when the Brotherhood kidnapped me. That I wanted to talk to Karl again, and I had convinced Sean, Sadie, Fynn, and Rodd to go with me—a white lie, for their sake. That Karl gave us the address of the place where the dark witches operated from, and I had convinced the others to go check it out. But the place seemed deserted, so we ventured inside—and found the ghosts and the strange vials. "So, we freed all the ghosts, including Doug, and brought one of the vials to be examined."

The witches listened to it all, their expression deadpan. If they thought I was crazy and should be expelled, I couldn't tell.

"I'll need to have a talk with my son," the queen said. "About lying in his reports."

"It's not his fault, Your Majesty," I added quickly. "I asked them do it. I ... I was afraid I would get in trouble and be expelled from the program. But it was all on me. The sneaking out, the plan's idea and execution, and the report. He did it because I insisted."

She watched me, her eyes impassive. "With the Brotherhood after you, you should have been more careful. Leaving the castle, even with two highly capable warriors and a powerful witch, is dangerous."

I took that as an opening. "Do you know why the Brotherhood is after me?"

The queen hesitated. "No, I don't. We don't."

Why did it sound like she was lying? It reminded me of what Shade had told me: Do not trust anyone.

"May I ask about the vial? What was that strange liquid inside it?"

"We still don't know," the queen said, her voice cold. "We have our best witches working on it as we speak."

For some reason, I knew that even if she found out, she wouldn't tell me.

I nodded. "Will I be punished for last night's events?"

Again, the queen looked before answering. "No, you won't. But we expect better from you next time. If something like this happens again, you are to come to us, and we'll help you."

Was she lying to my face again? It sounded like it.

"I—"

"One more thing," the queen said, cutting me off. "Starla, the dark witch you fought during your test, asked for you this morning. She said she needs to talk to you." I stilled. Queen Denise's eyes narrowed. "Any idea what that is about?"

I shook my head, hoping they couldn't see the panic rising inside of me. "No, I don't ... perhaps she sensed what I was up to? I mean, it all started with her."

"Perhaps," the queen muttered.

"Will you ... will you allow me to see her?"

"No."

I frowned. What if she had sensed what I had done, what I and the others had done? What if she wanted to yell at me, spew nonsense, but in the middle of all that, she let out some of her secrets? Why they were collecting ghosts, what they were doing with them?

But I wasn't about to argue with the witch queen. So, I shut up and nodded.

"You can go back to class now," the queen said.

"Yes, Your Majesty." I turned to get my things and leave.

Thunder echoed through the room.

With a yelp, I jumped when a flash of dark light cut from the ceiling where I had been standing a second ago. My heart in my throat, I took several steps back. The lightning struck three more times in the same spot, and dark flames spread across the floor, the scent of burnt rubber heavy in the air.

Around me, the council members stood from their

chairs, their eyes wide at the crackling flames that danced on the stone floor.

Finally, after several seconds, smoke rose from the flames, and they died out.

And on the floor was another rune.

I stared at it, trying to memorize it. This had to mean something, didn't it? I was sure it did ... but what?

"Grace, escort Miss Hazel to her bedroom," the queen ordered.

"But—"

"Of course." Grace sprang into action. Her green snake slithered around her chair and disappeared into the dark corners of the room. She clutched my upper arm and pulled me toward the doors. "Come, Hazel."

"Wait, but ..." But what? What did the lightning mean? What did the rune mean? Why was it slightly different from Arianna's? What weren't they telling us? Telling me? Had this happened before? When? How? Who was there?

But they wouldn't tell me anything. So, I grabbed my stuff from the chair and let Grace take me out of the room.

In the hallways, Light Order members ran toward the council room, and witches spied from other rooms. Apparently, everyone had heard the thunder.

"Everyone, back to their tasks!" Grace yelled. "Now!"

All the witches scurried out of the way, though a handful of Light Order members continued their trek to the council room.

I only noticed we had taken several different turns when we stepped into a large, industrial kitchen.

"Through here." Grace took me past a glass door and into what looked like a private dining room.

I glanced around to the long glass table and the cushioned chairs. "What is this place?"

"A small conference-slash-dining room. It's rarely used. Here." She pulled up a chair and gestured for me to sit. "I'll be right back."

She disappeared into the kitchen, and I sank into the chair, dropping my stuff on the chair next to me. I still didn't understand what was happening here. My brain had suddenly become sluggish, and I felt I was missing something.

There was a connection between all of this: the dark witches, the ghosts, the Brotherhood, the lightning, the runes. There had to be. Or I was trying to make them connect because I needed to solve them. I didn't like all the mess ensuing around me.

A moment later, Grace came back with a small silver tray with a cup of tea. "It's chamomile. For your nerves."

I took the cup and put it over the table. "I thought you were supposed to take me to my bedroom."

She took the chair to my left. "You seemed shocked, because of the lightning. I thought you could use some tea before resting."

"That's kind of you," I muttered. Grace seemed to always be looking out for me, taking care of me. I was glad and thankful for that. "Thanks."

"Don't mention it, dear." She patted my knee. "I want you to feel better."

I reached for the cup and drank a good sip of the tea. It was hot, but not too much, and it was sweet, the way I liked it. "Thanks," I said again.

She offered me a smile. "Anything for you."

13

THE REST OF THE DAY WAS SLOW AND QUIET. CLASSES AND mentoring for the initiates had been canceled, the full-fledged witches were busy, and half of the Light Order was patrolling the castle, while the other half was gone.

When dropping me off at my room Grace warned me to stay in the castle. With the Brotherhood on the loose and the dark witches' plans destroyed, they could be onto me more than ever.

I purposely went to dinner late, so I missed my group. I ate fast, all the while texting Sean.

> It's a shame my training starts next week.
> I want to be there with you now.

> I know. Me too.

Of course, I had told him what had happened—the council meeting, the lightning, and how boring the rest of the day was.

next week, though.

yeah, next week. I confess, it'll be hard to leave the dojang behind.

Sean, you can still change your mind.

My phone rang and I smiled. "Hey," I answered.

"I won't change my mind," Sean said, his tone serious.

Those words, those simple words ... they warmed my heart. "I'm glad."

We talked a little more, mostly about what he would tell his parents when he moved to the castle. He decided that until he passed the training and joined for real, he wouldn't say anything. He would freeze his enrollment in Towland, so they wouldn't be paying for nothing, but he would let them assume he was still going to classes and practicing Taekwondo.

If—when—he became a member of the Light Order, then he didn't know. He didn't want to lie to his parents, not about such a big thing, but at the same time, he knew he couldn't tell them the truth.

We talked late into the night; I fell asleep while on the phone with him.

"PRETTY, WEAK WITCH."

A shrill voice pierced through my dreams. At first, I thought it was just part of my dream.

"Wake up, witch."

I opened my eyes and came face-to-face with Starla. She hovered over me in bed, her long, dark, dirty hair around my face. Her foul breath washed over me.

I screamed.

She cackled as she jumped back and landed softly on the floor beside my bed, like a tiger. "I wanted to say thank you."

I sat up in bed, my eyes wide, my hands shaking, and tried making sense of the scene before me. My room was dark, except for the light coming from the large window, and there was a freaking dark witch in my room!

No, I was hallucinating. Or I hadn't truly woken up yet. This was a dream within a dream.

"F-for?" I asked. Slowly, I moved my arm and reached for my phone, which still rested on the pillow beside me. I hoped it wasn't drained of battery by now.

"I hope to meet you again soon," she said. She was still dirty, but now she wore a black cloak over her ragged prison clothes. "I'll be looking forward to that."

"What?"

I clutched my phone.

The witch whirled on her heels and dashed out of the room. With my phone in hand and looking for Fynn's number, I raced to the door. I spied out and saw the edge of a black cloak disappearing around the corner.

I pressed call on my phone as a thunder of footsteps rained down the hallway. At least a dozen of Light Order members rounded the opposite corner the witch had gone through. Upon seeing me, Fynn and Rodd slowed down.

"Hazel?"

"I was about to call you." I pointed to the other side of the corridor. "The witch. The dark witch. She was here. She went that way."

Fynn frowned. He and Rodd exchanged a glanced. Rodd nodded. Fynn called out to the other warriors, and they continued marching down the hall, after the witch.

By then, doors started opening and witches spied out.

"What's happening?"

"What's that noise?"

"I'm trying to sleep here."

Rodd took a step closer to me, forcing me to take a one back. I was fully inside my room now. "Just wait here."

"Wait? For what? Shouldn't you be tracking the witch?"

He stared at a random point above my head, and he didn't say anything.

Something was off here, and I had no idea what.

A moment later, Queen Denise, Lenora, and Clara appeared behind Rodd. Now, the hallway was crowded with witches who wanted to know what was going on.

I wanted to know too.

"Thank you, Rodd," the queen said.

He stepped aside and let the three witches enter my room. I retreated even more, suddenly conscious that I was wearing short shorts and a thin tank top—my usual pajamas—while the queen and the two council members were dressed in full gowns, jewelry, and makeup. Even their hair was in delicate updos.

At three in the morning?

They either never slept, or they knew a spell to get ready within seconds. I would like to know that spell too.

"Hazel Rose Levine," the queen started.

I stilled. "Y-yes?"

"It has come to our attention that you visited Starla last night," she said, her voice as sharp as her gaze. "Yesterday, she asked for you, and now she was spotted leaving your bedroom during her escape."

I gulped. "I'm sorr—"

"I don't want apologies, I want explanation. Were you aiding the dark witch or not?"

I faltered. "What? Of course not!"

"Then how do you explain why she was here, instead of simply escaping?"

"I ... I don't know."

She watched me for a moment with blank eyes. "Hazel, I like you. I've liked you since you first walked into the council room. I've put up with Moira's complaints, and several reports and letters on why you should be dismissed from the program. I personally invested and bet on your future here. If you have nothing to do with the witch's escape, then explain to me, why were you visiting her last night? And what was she doing here just now?"

"Last night, before going to search for Karl, my first idea was to talk to her," I said, afraid there was a ticking clock over my head. "I went to her to ask her about Doug and the other ghosts. Deep down, I knew she wouldn't tell me anything, but I had to try. As for now ... I don't know. She scared the shit out of me." I lifted my cell phone. "I was about to call Fynn to come after her when he showed up with the others."

Queen Denise looked at Lenora and Clara. Something I couldn't hear or see what passed between them.

"Hazel, you are confined to this bedroom until we find the witch, capture her, interrogate her ... and interrogate you," the queen announced. My breath caught. "Someone will bring you meals at appointed times, and there will always be two Light Order members outside. If you remember anything, if you want to confess, let them know."

She turned to leave.

"Wait ..." I called out. "I ... I didn't do anything."

The three witches didn't even acknowledge me as they walked out of my bedroom. I ran to her, almost clutched at the queen's hands, but stopped myself before I complicated the situation.

Rodd stood by the door after they left, and he gave me a pitiful look before closing the door on my face.

I stared at the door for a long time, stunned.

What the hell had happened?

Continue reading Hazel's adventures with book 4, *The Midnight Secret*!

BONUS: want to read an exclusive scene from Sean's POV? Download it here!

To read a special and exclusive book about another light witch, join my Facebook Group and find the book called *The Light Witch* to download on the "featured" tab!

THANK YOU

T<small>HANK YOU FOR READING</small> *T<small>HE</small> M<small>IDNIGHT</small> F<small>LAME</small>*!

Reviews are very important for authors. If you liked my book, please consider leaving a review on your favorite online retailer and/or on Goodreads and/or Bookbub, please!

D<small>ID YOU LIKE THIS BOOK?</small> Y<small>OU CAN CHECK OUT OTHER BOOKS</small> of mine:

The Night Calling (Rite World: Night Wolves book 1): she was abandoned by her mate, left in the hands of a terrible half-demon ... but now he's back and ready to claim her.

The Darkest Vampire (Rite World: Vampire Wars book 1): a witch releases a dark vampire from a curse, and becomes inadvertently bonded to him.

The Demon Kiss (Rite World: Blackthorn Hunters Academy book 1): a fast-paced story about a young woman who finds out she's a demon hunter, and the half-demon intent on protecting her against all evil.

The Vampire Heir (Rite World 1: Rite of the Vampire): a dark and mysterious paranormal romance about a vampire and a young woman with a secret.

The Warlock Lord (Rite World 4: Rite of the Warlock): a thrilling and kick-ass paranormal romance about a were-wolf and warlock.

The Wolf Forsaken (Rite World 7: Rite of the Wolf): a heat-wrenching tale about a lost wolf shifter and a fae princess on the run.

Heart Seeker (The Fire Heart Chronicles book 1): an urban fantasy series about a young woman who finds herself at the center of a mysterious supernatural world.

Destiny Gift (The Everlast Series book 1): a post-apocalyptic urban fantasy series about a young woman with a special power that can save the world.

DON'T FORGET TO SIGN UP FOR MY NEWSLETTER TO FIND OUT about new releases, cover reveals, giveaways, and more!

If you want to see exclusive teasers, help me decide on covers, read excerpts, talk about books, etc, join my reader group on Facebook: Juliana's Club!

ABOUT THE AUTHOR

While USA Today Bestselling Author Juliana Haygert dreams of being Wonder Woman, Buffy, or a blood elf shadow priest, she settles for the less exciting—but equally gratifying—life as a wife, a mother, and an author. She resides in North Carolina and spends her days writing about kick-ass heroines and the heroes who drive them crazy.

Subscribe to her mailing list to receive emails of announcement, events, and other fun stuff related to her writing and her books: www.bit.ly/JuHNL

For more information:
www.julianahaygert.com

facebook.com/julianahaygert

twitter.com/julianahaygert

instagram.com/juliana.haygert

goodreads.com/juliana_haygert

pinterest.com/julianahaygert

bookbub.com/authors/juliana-haygert

youtube.com/julianahaygert

tiktok.com/@julianahaygert

ALSO BY JULIANA HAYGERT

To find links and more info, go to:
www.julianahaygert.com/books/

The Soul Bond (Book 3)
The Shadow Trials (Book 4)
The Infernal Curse (Book 5)

Rite World
The Vampire Heir (Book 1)
The Witch Queen (Book 2)
The Immortal Vow (Book 3)
The Warlock Lord (Book 4)
The Wolf Consort (Book 5)
The Crystal Rose (Book 6)
The Wolf Forsaken (Book 7)
The Fae Bound (Book 8)
The Blood Pact (Book 9)

The Wyth Courts
Winter King (Book 1)
Spring Warrior (Book 2)
Summer Prince (Book 3)
Autumn Rebel (Book 4)

The Fire Heart Chronicles
Heart Seeker (Book 1)
Flame Caster (Book 2)
Earth Shaker (Book 2.5)
Sorrow Bringer (Book 3)
Soul Wanderer (Book 4)
Fate Summoner (Book 5)
War Maiden (Book 6)

The Everlast Series
Destiny Gift (Book 1)
Soul Oath (Book 2)
Cup of Life (Book 3)
Everlasting Circle (Book 4)

Willow Harbor Series

Hunter's Revenge (Book 3)
Siren's Song (Book 5)

<u>*Breaking Series*</u>
Breaking Free (Book 1)
Breaking Away (Book 2)
Breaking Through (Book 3)
Breaking Down (Book 4)

Made in the USA
Coppell, TX
16 March 2023